The Perfect Lesson

The Logic of Lust

By

Young Darby

authorHOUSE®

© 2004, 2014 by Young Darby. All rights reserved.

No part of this book may be reproduced, stored in a retrieval system, or transmitted by any means, electronic, mechanical, photocopying, recording, or otherwise, without written permission from the author.

ISBN: 978-1-4107-3848-6 (sc)
ISBN: 978-1-4107-3849-3 (e)

This book is printed on acid free paper.

1stBooks - rev. 12/06/05

Introduction

Real characters of strength, weaknesses, humility, integrity, wisdom as well as ignorance, inspired this book. I enjoyed doing this work, because not only is it based on truthful events that actually occurred, I personally know the characters whose names have been slightly changed to protect their privacy. The story is inspiring, thought provoking and delves into some of the various situations that confront us in life, especially the Christian.

This book explores the meaning of Christianity as well as what Christianity may mean individually as well as what it may mean in light of the Holy Bible. This book repeatedly challenges one to examine their walk with the Lord and their relationship with the Lord if any. To me this book is a critical reading that will provoke essential and critical thinking for the believing Christian. I wish that everyone who reads this book would write or email me with his or her comments. My e-mail has been provided for your feedback. Your thoughts are very important. You may not read this entire introduction because you probably can't wait to sink your eyes into the pages ahead. But just in case you do find time to read this, please drop me a line. Your feedback is very important to me and I need it. It would be a welcomed meal. Don't worry about the brand of comments, for I have also eaten bones before. They stick, but also teaches their own lessons. I thank God for keeping you and me so that we can both share in this wonderful journey ahead, because the journey ahead could not happen and would be impossible without you. If you are not a Christian, this book will give some great insight and understanding concerning the plight of many Christians (or at least those that call theirselves Christian) that you probably would have never imagined. This book also embarks on the controversy surrounding the issue or concept of perfection which tends to be the central topic of concern, for there are many Christians as well as Non-Christians that wrestle with the questions of perfection. Some even question the bible's request for man to be perfect by interpreting such a request to be misunderstood, or symbolic and unrealistic. Christians and Non-Christians draw these conclusions alike. On the other hand, lust is accepted as being normal and understandable without any controversy.

These and others issues are illuminated and addressed considerately and as mindfully as possible without suffering removal of the truth on which this story is based.

Please understand that since this novel is based on true events and situations, there were occasions where some profanities were used in keeping true to the actual events and situations.

Acknowledgements

I would like to thank God thru my Lord and Savior Jesus Christ for being so good to me and being my always present help and best friend who have always treated me perfectly in all of his dealings with me. And I would like to thank him again for Jesus. I also would like to thank Jesus for all of his suffering in which he suffered for me. I like to thank my mother, Ms. Bertha L. Darby (now in heaven) for her continued support and encouragement in all that I have attempted to do. A thanks to my wife, Sarah who supported me in every way especially during the writing of this work, for her kind words, Jallof rice and for being there for me whenever I needed help. And a special thank you to Gimra, Portia and Kaleb for working hard in school and doing most of their housework during this writing so that I could stay focussed enough to complete this work. I love you all.

A note to the reader: Over and over again the typo's has been corrected, but upon saving letters or characters and punctuations, these items has a tendency to be displaced during the internal mechanical saving process. If you find a coma or character displaced please try to over look, for during the saving process regardless of how many times an attempt is made to save all of the characters, some are inevitably lost just as it will be in the last days. But those characters will be where there is weeping and knashing of teeth. So I guess that these characters that's still hanging around though they are displaced and in the wrong place are still here because they were saved by grace.

Last but not least, I would like to take this time to thank everyone who buy and read this book. I hope that if you like it, you would tell a friend.

Chapter 1
The Perfect Lesson

"Hold it a minute Pastor, it's just us deacons here! We know that you are a great Christian and preacher and all. That's all good. And we know that some friends are good, some are bad, but that's life," one of the Deacons frankly replied.

"Well then: Point two", the Preacher continued, "I have found out what a true friend is and what a true Christian is, therefore I know what a Christian and a friend is not. Knowing these two things, allows me to understand how one would truly be blessed beyond one's imagination if anyone had simply one true friend in this world."

Being the impatient one, Deacon Giz interrupted the pastor, saying, "Pastor, I know where you heading, but I have quite a few loyal friends that would do anything for me. Thank God it's still some good folk left. You know what I mean?"

"I understand where you comin' from Deacon, but a friend of the devil can say the samething."

"Hold it Pastor, are you calling me a devil?"

"Oh certainly not. What I'm saying is, if one had one true friend, and that one friend just happened to be a Christian, in my opinion the benefits of having that one friend would more than equal the benefits of what one may receive from a thousand so-called friends, in and of this world."

"So what's your point Pastor? Got no friends?" said Deacon Giz. And the other deacons began chuckling.

Understanding the humor, the pastor gracefully smiled and continued: "My friends, if you were to search your heart and your circle of relationships, you would probably discover that out of the thousands of conversations and small talks, laughs, jokes and confiding moments you spent with significant others, you really don't have a friend in this world yourself. You probably haven't met more than one real Christian in your entire life."

Being a little confused, Deacon Mark interjected, "Well Pastor, tell you the truth, I have quite a few friends myself that would do anything for me as well. If I had a need, I could always count on one of them to meet it. So that may not apply to everyone, huh?"

The pastor momentarily stared at Mark, and then proceeded, "I hear what you're saying, but I'm not talking about someone that you call a friend or who calls theirselves your friend, or call theirself a Christian because they once visited you or somebody else in the hospital: lent you or someone else a few dollars, goes to church, and/or reads the Bible. But a real Christian in lifestyle, character, in consistent honesty, with consistent Christ-like

The Perfect Lesson

behavior. One who is endeavoring to walk in Jesus Christ's footsteps.

Not someone who believes that everyone must sin sometimes because they can't help him or herself. Shucks! You may also discover that you yourself is not a friend to anyone."

In reading the assembled deacon's body language, Pastor Gateway could see that the deacons were growing indifferent to his suggestions, for they thought of themselves as genuine Christians, and men of God, but the pastor's signaled with his hands, thus, buffeting their bodily expressions, that he was not finished and continued artfully expressing his point with his hands and head movements as only he could do, saying, "My Fellow Deacons, some of you may even call yourself a Christian, knowing deep down inside, you're not! Knowing that you too have no intentions of trying to walk in Jesus footsteps or even as he walked. For the most part, you are also so-called typical Christian. Like those who believe that going to church on Sundays' is enough but will not go on any other day if it would interfere with your schedule. These types of church-goers occasionally reads the Bible and only talks to the people they know about this person called, Jesus."

"Ok Pastor, but what do you want us to do? We aint perfect," Deacon Giz replied.

"That's my point Deacon."

Young Darby

"What point is that?"

"The truth is, we're not really interested in raising the dead, the laying on of hands and seeing instantaneous and miraculous healings, interpreting tongues, having a routine active part in souls being saved, walking perfectly before God, and allowing ourselves to be translated from any place on earth to another place from time to time. We might as well admit it my fellow Deacons, we know these have not been our aspirations, but correct me if I'm wrong. We are not yet walking in Jesus footsteps. Oh yes, we could if we really wanted to. But I'm afraid that we don't want to. I'm afraid that we just don't feel like it. I'm afraid that we also believe that we can't. Cause if somebody is walking as Jesus walked, some, or all of these super natural things should be happening on a daily basis or with some degree of regularity in some form or another even with our knowledge: and if occurring rarely, they should be regularly rarely occurring manifestations in our life and in this ministry. It's time for all of us to get on the ball gentlemen."

What's A True Friend?

The assembled deacons began to grow even more weary and some even became offended, especially Giz. Only Deacon Mark and Deacon Kenney seemed interested in what was being said.

The Perfect Lesson

The Pastor went on: "Point number three. One may say, 'How do I be a friend?' I would answer that, this way."

"Yeah Pastor! Just how would you answer that? Because I really believe I know how to be a friend to someone. If you're born again, it should just come naturally," said Deacon Giz, interrupting the pastor like he was tired and had an appointment to go to.

Agreeing with deacon Giz, the other deacons said, "Amen."

The pastor continued, "Simply put brothers, you can't really be a friend to anyone if you don't believe in, and practice the Holy Bible from start to finish, but only believe and practice the parts that you like and that describes you to your own liking—— Huh, this don't make you a true friend. And even if you are living on your best behavior, and giving as much as you could possibly afford in your view to a needy person or to someone who appears to be homeless or to some organization, you still would not qualify as a genuine friend. However, in the world's eyes you would indeed be a friend and a Christian on the day that you gave because the world wants only what it can 'milk' out of you. And when there is no more 'milk', 'the same ones that you have been giving to, no longer want you."

Young Darby

"How can you say that about a homeless person, Pastor?" Deacons Giz asked.

"Don't ya' know that your typical homeless acting person would also turn his back on you on the day that you stop giving to him as well?" the Pastor replied.

"Maybe, but I don't think the organizations for the homeless would do that," Deacon Giz said, "because they are in it for the long-haul with a mind to serve. It takes a certain type of person to do that kind of work. Everybody just aint cut out for that. You have to really want to serve, that's all I'm saying Pastor."

"Point well taken Deacon, but now that you mentioned it, when is the last time you heard of any organization that's always taking in money for the poor, making donations to plain old families like yours or to you, or to just plain old hard working single parent families, and senior citizens with reduced incomes, barely making it after a lifetime of contributions?"

"I don't know," the deacon replied.

With attitude, the pastor continued, "Chances are, they will never ever get one brown cent from them, nor will you get a penny from them, nor will anyone else you know that needs help. The only ones reportedly helped by them are unknown people most of the time. People that you or I may

The Perfect Lesson

never meet or see in person for the most part in our entire lifetime."

"But Pastor, what do you want us to do about this, if they provide pictures of poor, naked and hungry children?" asked Mark.

"Well?" the pastor asked back.

"What do you think they are doing with the money?" Mark asked, as if demanding the answer.

"First of all, we have enough poor and underserved citizens right here in our own back yard, and as for the money, do you really want to know what they are doing with the money? Then look at their gorgeous buildings, furnishings, fleets of vehicles, and pay scale. And look again, no changes in the causes the money were claimed to have been collected for.

One famous U.S. performer responsible for delivering funds to Africa during the 'We Are The World We Are The Children Campaign', said that she did use part of the funds that was collected for the needy children for herself to travel in first class to deliver such funds, and upon reaching there did stay in the most choice hotel and added that, that was what she was accustomed to. And I'm sure you know about that, so now let us just reason for a moment.

Wouldn't you think that when organizations are raising millions of dollars each year in the name of the disadvantaged, or even in the name

Young Darby

of Jesus, their would be enough allocated over a three to four year period of time or sooner to create a regenerating financial mechanism whereby permanent independence on some level is achieved via an investment vehicles of some type regardless of any possible tax consequences? Hey! If the money is there, pay the taxes too while you at it.

If keeping your non-profit status is the issue, setup trust funds for the disadvantage and needy that you are really saying that you are tryin' to help and raise funds for. But yet look at the lavish churches and ministries supposedly erected in the name of Jesus, with no meat in them. For this was the only thing really established, soft and plush dwellings for the caretakers of these gifts and offerings. Now it seems that everyone wants to build the biggest and fanciest church edifice and be paid for looking after it.

And I must add, that we know of a few large ministries that have turned their members away who needed a helping hand when the times got hard. Then they blamed the members for not having enough faith. Even preaching that it's their lack of faith, while calling them 'brother and sister'! Saying, 'You must claim it like I did'. Go ahead, you be the judge. My Bible says that you don't need a great deal of faith. All you need is faith the size of a mustard seed, but when a bill need to be paid you need money. Go visit a few local

The Perfect Lesson

churches in your neighborhood, and ask for a piece of bread for a family. You may learn that a lot of churches don't even keep enough food on hand to feed one family or enough money on hand to pay one member's rent without taking a major vote and a special collection." The Preacher paused. Then proclaimed:

"One last thing Deacons, and I'll be on my way."

The preacher looked up, while folding his hands together like he was praying and said, **"Yes! Lord, I love everyone. Have mercy Jesus. I Love you Lord today.** Does this sound familiar Deacons? And notice that this same person is still lying, cheating, conniving, fornicating, committing adultery and can't wait to cheat.

And is still speaking out against sin in the church. This individual prays to God out of his mouth but his eyes are still filled with adultery, and a heart full of lust. He can't wait to sin. Don't really want to stop sinning. It feels too good to quit. But 'Halleluiah, I love the Lord with all of my heart, soul, and mind and strength,' they say. With hands lifted high while giving outward praises and exaltations to our wonderful Lord and Savior. Face filled with all solemnity. From time to time even uttering in other tongues and singing great hymns, such as, 'I surrender all'. Yet shacking-up, cheating, and deep down inside feel that it's OK

Young Darby

for now, because all he or she have to do is ask for forgiveness and cry a few tears and sing a song and shout, 'Glory'.

I'm sorry Deacons, I lied I need two more minutes.

"Wait a minute Pastor! Just wait one-minute right there. I still don't see where ya' driving to. You still haven't told us why you brought us out here," Deacon Giz objected.

"I'm coming Deacon! Just hold on for two more minutes I'm almost there," the Pastor said as he lifted his preaching voice and went on, "Now Jesus said, if you love me, you would keep my word. Then he went on to say, 'We are to be perfect *as our Father in Heaven is also perfect'*. But we so-called Christians resort to the world's way of disputing God's word by saying, 'He really didn't mean it. We can't be perfect man. No one can be perfect,' we say!"

The head deacon, Deacon Zeek, in his favorite charcoal pinstriped three piece worsted wool: the only one not in a plain black suit or in uniform today, though in deep thought, could no longer hold his peace, slowly stepped forward.

He was the stocky short one, well known for his intellectualism, biblical and scientific research as well as his unusual ability to teach and get a point across.

The Perfect Lesson

He stepped out from the group of the assembled deacons and spoke up: "I beg your pardon Pastor! I believe what Jesus meant was, for us to be perfect in our intentions, and I believe that I share the opinions of all the brothers here today. By you having Christ living in you, you're made perfect on the inside, cause you see, can't nobody really be perfect like the Bible seems to be indicating or directing from one glance. You know that! Come on Pastor.

We weren't meant to be perfect. Now I can see if you said we should do our best. But be perfect! No way. We were born in sin and shaped in inequity so how can a sinful man or women turn around and be perfect? Even after you're born again, you're still gonna sin. Most of the time you don't even have to be thinking about anything, and a sinful thought would just pop up in your mind. That aint our fault. We can't help it when these thoughts just come up.

Even though Jesus came as a man, and lived as a man and even though the Bible said he was perfect as a man as he lived as a man without sin or fault, that don't apply to us. Cause he was different. He was 'The' Son of God. We are the sons of man. He was, 'The' Anointed One. We were made from dirt. He always was."

Young Darby

"Yeah, he was made by the spirit but he was still born of flesh in the womb of Marry, but go ahead," the pastor said.

"Now, now, I know the word says he was coming back for a church without spot or blemish, and directly tells us to be perfect. But the God of heaven really didn't mean it that way, because if he did, we would not have to be tried and tested so much. Though the scripture says, 'whosoever committed sin transgressed the law also: for sin is the transgression of the law......' And I understand the part that says, 'Whosoever abide in him does not sin...' Yes! I know it says all of this, as well as, 'He that committed sin is of the devil.' But what you must understand preacher, is that when *you* become perfect, its time for you to go away from here my friend, because what are you doing down here perfect anyway? So don't worry about it. Jesus really didn't mean it when he said it like that. He meant it figuratively, in another way."

"Well, what did he really mean Deacon?" the pastor then asked. "So it's Ok to send a little?"

"Yeah! Well—-No! Well—-just let me say this. From my in-debt analysis of the antinomiological ramifications of perfection, Jesus meant for us to be perfect within our spirit-man. He knows that we gonna keep on sinning, because you see, he said himself, that the flesh is week, and that offences 'must' come. And that's the way we were made."

The Perfect Lesson

"You really believe that Deacon?" the pastor asked, looking at the other deacons.

"Pastor, ma—-n, I sin just about everyday, don't you?" Deacon Zeek replied.

The pastor did not respond, but Giz and a few of the other deacons, 'high fived' each other in agreement.

Deacon Zeek continued, "He knows we can't be perfect. *He just said it figuratively*. Don't take it serious, or as it is written, cause you know as well as I, the bible is full of many symbolisms, parables and mysteries and one man can't figure it all out. I know it says, 'Be perfect', but let's face it, all of us here have done some kind of sin since this morning, even up to the Pope, but God aint going to take heaven from us for that. We just ask him to forgive us and we just keep' on keepin' on."

The assembled deacons in full agreement, sounded a harmonious and resounding,

"A—-men". Deacon Zeek paused, took a commanding breath assured he had won the debate, slightly gritted his teeth, placing both hands on his waist, shrugged his shoulders, confidently swayed his head back and continued even in a more smoother and confident manner: "You see Sir, his grace is sufficient and covers-up all of our past, present and future sins."

And again the elders and Deacon harmoniously went, "A—-men," except for deacon Mark, and

Young Darby

Kenney who were the only ones taking notes as was the norm for them, especially when in the middle of a debate, they would go and study the matters in light of the scripture.

Mark was a fairly new member and deacon but was best known for his sincerity to the work of the ministry and visiting and praying for the sick and the shut-in. He was about 5ft 8, with a thin built, light golden brown complexion and wore small circular eyeglasses and wore a Philly hairstyle. Kenney was a little shorter and darker and well known for his work with foster kids.

Chapter 2
(Who can be perfect?)

Pastor Gateway, responded, "Oh! So what are you saying?"

"Um saying that you don't have to be perfect."

"Is it that you don't want to become perfect because you might have to go be with the Lord sooner?"

Speaking for the deacons, Deacon Giz said, "We are not saying neither."

The pastor continued: "Well are you sayin' it's Ok to sin because its' inevitable?"

"In a way," said Giz pulling on his collar while looking at Deacon Zeek.

"Or, are you saying, Jesus deliberately told us to do something he knew we couldn't do?"

"I didn't say that," Giz replied.

"Or maybe, you are saying, he knew we would figure it out sooner or later, that we could not really be perfect regardless of his command or instruction."

With squinting stares, the deacons looked at each other as the pastor stared them down awaiting an answer. Now, all of a sudden they seem to have been in a thinking mode or in an examining mode. The pastor abruptly continued with a sudden look of surprise on his face, did an about-face, turning and facing the head Deacon with out-stretched hands, with piercing eyes as if he just received the answer, saying, "If we are already made perfect in our spirit after accepting Christ, as some would suppose, why are we as well as they:

the apostles, commanded to continue and to be yet perfect and to hold fast until the end?

And if we hold not fast we shall not receive the promise."

Deacon Giz attempted to answer, "But…"

Cutting him off, the pastor said, "If we are already made perfect in our spirit man just by receiving him, what can change us? Why do we have to hold fast? Why do we have to endure?"

Again Deacon Giz tried, "Well…"

"Can something change us?" the pastor said cutting in again.

"No, I don't think anything could change you if you are already perfect because you're perfect," Deacon Zeek rifled.

"Well why did he say hold fast then, if nothing could change us? Oh Deacons! What are you saying? How are you believing?"

Deacon Zeek came one step closer to Pastor Gateway. Looking down while shaking his head and smiling in disbelief, revealing his brilliant white teeth, and glancing back at the assembly of elders and again at the pastor while folding his

The Perfect Lesson

arms in front of his chest, looked up, smiled and said, "Well, Pal', I'm not ready to go *yet* either, are you? He..he..he..He," he said quietly grinning, "And plus, I never saw a perfect person in this world. *Have you*? Now tell the truth? Can you name one person that even came close to being perfect, besides Jesus?"

Pastor Gateway, paused for a moment and then went on, "Well, really, I don't know if I have or have not seen or met a perfect person. But I do know one thing. And that's this."

The pastor continued while clinching his fist with his finger briefly pointing and shaking it towards the deacon's nose.

"I have not seen a big enough representative fraction of *all* the people of *the entire* world nor have I spoken to such as to come to such a conclusion. In-fact, there are more people that I have not seen or spoken to in this world, then those that I have seen and spoken with.

In this light, to me, it would be narrow minded, self-centered, hypocritical, stereo-typical, foolish and prejudice of me to say that if the few people that I have met and know something about in my short journey here are not a certain way or are perfect before God, *no one else is, or could be, or would be.* Who am I to judge the world?

No Deacons. I dare not to make such an assumption or accusation. Because even I believe

Young Darby

that even right now living on this planet, there are others smarter, wiser, and sharper than I, and probably have more love being expressed in them than I. So what about those that may be wiser or lovelier then they, and more careful than those, and so-forth? Therefore, if I knew and met ten million people, my sample would still be too small compared to *all* the people that are presently in this world alive, and those that once lived and those that are to come. But by the way, in the small sample of people I do have some knowledge of, is it ok to include: Moses, and Daniel, Caleb, Shedrack, Meshack, Ebendego, Isaac, David, Joab, Abraham, A'sa, Job, King Solomon, Esther, Noah, Mohamed, Oh, and John, Helen, Martha, Mary, Elizabeth, Naomi, Ruth, Esther, Enoch, Elijah, Peter, Paul, and James, Harriet Tubman, M. Gandhi. And the man they called Mandela.

And how about the man that love manifest itself into a open view of perfection, who was called Martin Luther King Jr. while in our day, not long ago, before those that did not believe in perfection in this society and equal rights, who assassinated him. If my memory serves me right, you even had the privilege of meeting him. Like Jesus, he saw it coming and therefore preached his own funeral which me and you heard together.

Moreover the book of Hebrews informs us also of those who through faith subdued kingdoms,

The Perfect Lesson

wrought righteousness, obtained promises, stopped the mouth of lions, quenched the violence of fire, escaped the edge of the sword, out of weakness was made strong, waxed valiant in fight, turned to flight the armies of the aliens. Women received their dead raised to life again: and others were tortured, not accepting deliverance; that they might obtain a better resurrection: And others had trials of cruel mockings and scourgings and imprisonment. They were stoned, they were sawn asunder, were tempted, were slain with the sword: they wandered about in sheepskin and in goatskins, being destitute, afflicted and tormented. They wandered in deserts, in mountains and in dens and in caves of the earth. The bible said that the world was not even worthy of them.

These people were actually deemed by God to be too good for this world. And these all, having obtained a good report through faith, did not even receive the promise. God having provided some better thing for us, that they, even though they went through all that they did go through, without us should not be made perfect. So, I just don't think I'm qualified to judge such as these or anyone else for that matter.

Nevertheless, just to mention a few of the ones that I do know something about is enough to make me believe that perfection is what the Lord is looking for in us. I'm not saying all of these were perfect at all times.

However, they were close enough to make me believe, that they at least believed in perfection in its rawest state.

They also proven, a pure heart to serve the living God of heaven to the extent that our God who is in heaven held them up in high esteem and found them worthy enough to engrave their names and experiences into his holy word, which we are commanded to study and live by. And some of them he did say in plan language, were perfect. And those, I believe were just plain perfect even as the word of God said.

Yes! And even among the small amount of people that I have met and know in my present life, even now, [the pastor said while looking at Mark] from time to time, I've observed a person or two who are in my absolute opinion are after the very heart of Christ, and because of their righteous lifestyle, even though I'm a preacher, I'm often convicted, edified, instructed, strengthen, built-up, rejuvenated, percolated, motivated, regenerated, charged-up, and challenged by them to strive at peak performance at each rising sun until it's setting, for my Lord and Savior, Jesus Christ. Halleluiah!

Yes, I believe in perfection, even though I never been completely perfect myself. Nevertheless

The Perfect Lesson

there are times more often then before, that I do experience moments of perfection in my walk.

Yes! And I'm striving to lengthen the duration of these wonderful experiences, moment-by-moment and day-by-day. Oh! How I wish the Lord would come back at such a time and catch me walking upright and perfectly. To some degree I'm experiencing it right now. Hallelujah!"

"Ok! Ok! All that sound cool Pastor, but who can be purely perfect at all times?" Deacon Giz asked insistently.

"You can! I Can! Anyone can," the pastor responded. "Whosoever will can be perfect, spotless from sin and without blemish as a man or woman. Who do you think Jesus is coming back for, the spotted or the blemished?

"Neither Pastor!"

"The Blemished?"

"Nope."

"How about the defeated?"

"I see what ya sayin'."

"Well how about non-believers Deacon Giz?"

Deacon Giz started shaking his head like it was enough and that he understood what Gateway point was.

"Or maybe those that don't believe that God has been straight with them?"

No one answered the pastor this time and the pastor in his raged continued:

Young Darby

"Yes we all have sinned, but after we accepted Christ we suppose to stop sinning on purpose doggon'it. We suppose to stop and live holy without sin at some point in our life, don't we? We suppose to live clean and holy. We don't suppose to continue to walk in sin. We suppose to be walking in Jesus footsteps, right?

We should be walking and behaving and talkin' just like Jesus. Regardless of how we physically look. When someone meets us, they should say, 'He or She is just like Jesus.'"

"But Pastor…." cried Deacon Giz.

But the pastor continued, "Haven't you studied the letters of John, Deacon Giz?"

"Yes I did…"

"Then you should know that since we are still in the flesh, if we sin, it should be by sudden mistake only. We should not do any premeditated sin. If we walk in the spirit, we would not fulfill the lust of the flesh. And we walk in the spirit by keeping our mind always on his words and on what he wants us to do, because his word is spirit, and life and the light. So if we walk in his word we would be automatically walking in the spirit of Christ, which is also the spirit of God and we would be one with the Father and with the son. All Christians must stop sinning———-point blank!"

Deacon Zeek with his hands to his chest, palms facing the pastor, candidly replied, "I agree pastor,

The Perfect Lesson

but how come I'm not perfect, spotless and without blemish?"

"Oh that's an easy question Zeek! Its' because you're like me Deacon! You don't want to be perfect right now, for your own selfish and self-seeking and sinful foolish reasons. You just don't want to be perfect right now, and you don't want to do right. You enjoy your sin."

Deacon Zeek looked around at the other deacons as if he was a little shocked and offended, and said, "What in the …"

Deacon Giz agreeing with deacon's Zeek's expression, smirked and shook his head. Pastor Gateway stared into the deacons eyes and said, "But don't worry, there are many false people in the world who profess to be Christians that love in word and in tongue, that say that they *love everyone and that they love God*, but like me and you, they deliberately lie and don't keep his word because they just don't want to. In fact, in not keeping his word, we show that we really don't love him at all anyway, and is actually lying. And we lie every time we say we love him. That's right, we are telling him a great big old fat gigantic lie every time we open our big ungodly mouth and say that we love him. Don't worry, you're not alone, just about everyone you know are telling a great big fat lie just like you and me when they say that they love God. Then they demonstrate that they don't love him by not

Young Darby

keeping his word and even disagreeing with his word and would swear on a stack of Bibles that we don't have to be perfect like God word says."

"What?" Deacon Zeek shot back, holding his head with both hands, then searching the eyes of the other deacons for support, then leaning forward with out-stretched hands in disbelief as he looked on all with wide eyes as if he could not believe what he have just heard. "Hold it man! I can't believe you just said that I don't love God. I know I do. Maybe you don't, and maybe some of these deacons out here don't love God, but I......"

The pastor interrupted him: "Look Deacon, you don't have to lie to me, I don't have no heaven or hell to put you in.

You just said that Jesus didn't mean what he said. Are you saying he deceived us with those instructions to be perfect?"

"No," Zeek shot back.

"Did he lie to me?"

"No! I'm not saying that he lied at all."

"Then what are you saying?"

"All um saying is that I know I love God."

"Even though you don't keep his word all the time, right?"

"But just hold it for a minute and just pretend that you are right, how in the world we suppose to make it to heaven like this then, if what you are saying is total truth? Cause it seems like you're

The Perfect Lesson

saying that if we are not perfect, we wont make it to heaven!"

"Well?" the pastor replied while searching Zeek's eyes.

"But Pastor, you're not perfect. We here deacons don't claim to be perfect." The deacons agreeing with Zeek, went, "Amen to that brother."

"Uh huh. I see," the pastor said as he thought on the intent of what Zeek was saying.

Zeek looked at the Pastor as if he was waiting for him to say more. But instead of Gateway speaking, there was a space of silence of 30 seconds or more.

Annoyed by the silence and the pastor's apparent contentment with not saying anymore, Zeek asked, "So if this is true, if God really meant what he said, what do we do then? I know I love the Lord! And don't you?"

In a cool and confident manner the Pastor, explained, "The first thing we must do, is to stop saying the Bible does not mean what it says, that is, if we totally believe it.

As far as who is, and who is not going to live forever in the Kingdom of God when this mess is all over down here, all that is in the Lords hands. He will judge according to his goodness, even those that don't know him or never knew him like we were given the benefit of. So don't be surprise when you meet those in the Kingdom that you never saw attending, what you call the Christian Church.

Young Darby

I even suppose that there will be many that did not know of the miracle of Jesus that will enter into the Kingdom, as well as many that knew of the miracle of him, that will be cast in to hell's fires. Where there will be weeping and knashing of teethes and a great stink, Deacons. It's so simple to understand if we believe that the Bible is, 'The Word of God'. You see Deacons; we must accept it as we clearly understand it and even as it speaks to our hearts, even at our current level of understanding. For instance, if the Bible says we should not commit fornication, we should not somehow come to the conclusion that its alright to do it just because our so-called friends are doing it. Because those that's doin' this, are not really our friends.

To do this, is to compound sin. It would be wiser to tell the truth if we believe in God's word and confess that we are still miserable sinners and not Christians yet, but would like to become Christians. And we should confess that we are sorry for trying to make people think that we are Christians. And stop pretending that we are Christians while we are around certain people, and let Jesus know that we will not impersonate a Christian again, or simply tell Jesus that we are just not ready to live right at this time, but still want to be saved or considered as a candidate for salvation; and that we want to enter into his everlasting kingdom which shall thrive for ever and ever in paradise without end under his

The Perfect Lesson

magnificent rule, glory and splendor, honor and leadership.

Now gentlemen, we know that we have fornicators and adulterers in our church. And they call themselves Christians, but God don't call them Christians.

He calls them fornicators, and adulterers even if they come to church every Sunday in suits or robes, kenta-cloth, hair-ties, or come praying, preaching or singing. Just like you deacons: you can fool me but you can't fool God. Everybody that says that they are a Christian is not a Christian, point blank."

"Hold it Pastor. What did I do?"

"Excuse me?"

"Did I do somethin'?"

"Like what?"

"Did I try to fool you?"

"You're missing the point. You see, even if we are not perfect yet, we still can be honest right at the place that we are. As you know, God hates a liar. And a liar will have no part in the Kingdom of God. Since God hates liars, I believe that God loves those that tell the truth and are honest even if they have not accepted Christ yet. And if I'm honest, having no deceit in me and loves the truth, though not always perfect as he commanded yet, God may show me his sweet tender mercies and help me to become perfect and as he would have me to be."

Chapter 3
The Perfect Piece

"In other words Deacons, If you are fornicating, or committing adultery and you still call yourself a Christian or a born-again Believer, please don't tell your partner in fornication that you are a Christian. Not only would you be lying, you would also be bringing shame to the Household of God. Because God knows and you know that you are one of the worlds biggest liars on a straight path to hell if you are fornicating and saying you are a Christian. I know that none of you here are doing such things. I'm using the word, 'you', in the plural, for an example. Dig where I'm comin' from?"

"Uh huh," said Zeek.

"So then, my fellow brothers of the faith, be truthful, be faithful, be steadfast, and determined to be real with God. I read that God hate a liar and again I read that a fornicator will not inherit the Kingdom of Heaven. I don't know which is worse, a fornicator or a liar. Which one would you say is worse?"

"Beats me," said Giz.

Gateway looked out at all the deacons and asked, "Which will the fire burn the most?"

The Perfect Lesson

Some said they didn't know. Some agreed that fire was fire. Deacon Zeek paused for a moment thinking on the direction in which he thought the pastor was leading next and responded, "Now Pastor I understand where you comin' from, but you know as well as I, that nearly 100% of all the people attending church that are able, especially in our church, are committing premeditated fornication, and adultery on a regular basis, are hooked on cigarettes, some on booze, some on weed, some are gender confused, and who knows what else, and yet, would swear on a stack of Bibles that they done no wrong. If you preach this stuff, you better find another pulpit or job on stand-by, because the people here aint gonna wanna hear it. As for myself, I know I'm gonna have to find another job——- So is this why you called this meeting out here away from the church?"

Deacon Giz cut in, "Well I see why he called this meeting out here in the field now, because if the people heard this, ma——n, I know they'll think somethin' is wrong with us.

And please don't start talking about its wrong to play the 'One Arm bandit', because about half of the church visit him just about every week, especially sister Shirley. Man, she'll walk a mile for a slot and be talkin' about how much faith she got at the same time. That's her favorite spot! Yeah,

Young Darby

I see why you called it out here. If this leaked out, that'll be it."

Deacon Mike added, "I don't know about this. I'm gonna just follow y'all lead. I know I aint perfect, but I'm not saying I can't be. I just want to do what God requires of me. I'm in this race for the long haul. Know what I'm sayin'?"

"Me too," said Deacon Larry, "whatever y'all say 'bout being right with God, um goin' along with it, cause one day he's comin' back and he's gonna hold all of us accountable, especially you pastor."

"Well what do you have to say about this matter, Deacon Charles?" Gateway asked.

"Tell you the truth Rev, I don't think you have to be perfect. I agree with Giz and Zeek.

I believe when you mess-up or sin, all you have to do is ask God for forgiveness and he will forgive you. Then you try not to make that same mistake again. But if you do, thank God, he will forgive you again. So no matter how many times you make a mistake, he just gonna keep on forgiving you as long as you ask for forgiveness from your heart," Charles replied, rubbing his head.

"Deacon June?"

"Well sir, I don't know, I need more time to think and meditate about this. As far as being perfect is concern? I don't know. I really don't know if we can just be perfect as people, and always

The Perfect Lesson

do what's right. I think you gonna do something wrong once in a while. It's just human nature to do something wrong or to make a mistake. You could even experiment with something, thinking that it's alright, and it could be wrong. I think to be perfect, also mean to think perfect, which mean that you would always be perfect once perfect because you're thinking perfect. But that's my view off the cuff. Like I said, I need more time to study this piece."

"Deacon Calvin, what you say?"

"Well Pastor: Yes! And: No! Yes, because it's right. No, because it's impossible to be perfect all the time. I'm not saying that we shouldn't try to be perfect. But I guess I'm sayin' it's a growing and learning process. But God did say with him nothing is impossible, so it's just asking a lot. Man, it's asking a lot. But yet, it is still possible with God in my view, but yet, practically impossible."

"Deacon Kenney?"

"Well sir, God said that we should be perfect point blank. The way I see it, we should be perfect and we could be perfect if we really wanted to be. It could be done if we were to stay alert at all times in listening to his word, reading his word and staying in prayer and fasting often. Yeah. I believe it can be done. It's a matter of choice, and exercising our will, being focussed and determined. And with much prayer and fasting, we could achieve

Young Darby

it, but it would still be according to our individual abilities and level of understanding. However, the level of perfection achieved, may not be absolute, but relative to the understanding level of each individual Christian at a given point in time of one's Christian development."

Deacon Mark spoke up, "Well if the pastor is saying what is written, and we know it's written, then who can stand against it? How can we debate it? I believe he's telling it like it is. Jesus did say, 'Be perfect!' Maybe it's true, that we just don't want to be."

Deacon Zeek started to show that he was growing more disturbed now, because he liked Mark, but by Mark's ongoing body language and remarks, he was behaving like he had made-up his mind to go along with the pastor. So Zeek suggested, "Pastor, why don't you just preach that we all fall *short*? You don't have to get into what the *short* is all about. People know when they are sinning and who they're sinning with. I bet if we start preaching about perfection, immediately, tithes and offering are gonna drop or stop. Nobody gonna wanna come to church and hear it, I'm telling you Rev——. We gonna end-up, begging for financial miracles like them other TV and radio churches.

And before long you gonna be preaching to the chairs, begging for money, selling chicken dinners, socks, meat loafs and both of us still have families

The Perfect Lesson

to feed: and I haven't seen a loaf and a fish feeding 5000 lately either. Have you Pastor?"

"Can't say that I have Deacon."

"So shucks man! They already think they are doing us a favor when they just come to church. You see how sister Wiggi and her crew be sucking up their noses and clinching their purses at eleven o'clock service because of how big their offerings are. Come on man, they know 'we be' counting on it. And you telling me that you are gonna stand-up there and tell them that they are not real Christians and that they should strive to be perfect as the Father in Heaven is perfect? —— I don't think so. If you do, you might as well call them all, Impersonators, hypocrites, impostors and whatever else you can think of. And while you're at it, tell them they got a one way ticket to hell if they don't hurry-up and become perfect."

With gleaming and penetrating eyes Gateway, said nothing as he rubbed his slightly bearded chin, looking off into the distant rolling grassy plains, and beyond them, watching the trafficking of motor vehicles racing back and fourth. Then a cloud of pollution formed in the sky and hung in view. The cloud of pollution also caught the deacons' eye's. Feeling uneasy with this moment of silence, the Deacon went on,

"So Pastor, do you think we still may have a chance to get to Heaven even though we are not

Young Darby

perfect, or with a few spots and blemishes, if God really want us to be totally perfect as you say? But, at the same time believing and trusting in God?'

Becoming a little annoyed, Gateway replied, "Believing and trusting in God for what, Zeek? For just what we can get out of him? Ma—-n, I can believe that a sinner is gonna pay me back what I lent him, and when he repay me, he is still a sinner going to Hell!"

Deacon Giz, stepped in, "So what are you trying to say, Pastor? That we just stand-up and tell everybody in church to try to be perfect regardless if we're not? Just tell them that they should be trying to walk just like Jesus? That's what you want us to do?"

"I'm saying, that even sinners believe in God and are going to hell just the same. Saying that you believe is not enough."

"But Rev....," Zeek replied.

Gateway cut him off, "You know for yourself, Zeek, God want the real-thing. We just gonna have to do more than just be believing and trusting in God in order to make it into the Kingdom of Heaven."

"Hold it Pastor: with all due respect, can I be real and say what's on my mind?"

"Nothing never hindered you before!"

So Zeek went on, "Well, I think you are a little bit off right there about us having an obligation to do more than just believing and trusting God,

The Perfect Lesson

because the Word said all you have to do is believe and trust in the Lord. Now I know I'm at least right about that."

Gateway tightens his lips and held his peace.

"You're aint sayin', that aint true, are ya'?" Giz asked, being supportive of Zeek.

"You're right Deacon, the Word does says that. It says that quite clearly doesn't it?"

With a hint of glowing confidence, Zeek retorted, "Oh Yes it *certainly* does! So why are you sayin' that that's not enough then?"

"No! I agree with you."

"Ok then."

"Now Deacon Zeek, do the word also *certainly* says, be ye perfect as your Father in Heaven is also perfect?

"Sure Pastor"

"And what does *perfect* in that statement means to you?"

"I guess it means *perfect*."

"You guess?"

"Well you see Pastor, I don't know for sure."

"What you mean you don't know for sure?"

"I don't know!"

"You still know how to read, don't ya'?"

"Pastor, come on now!"

No! No! No! No!

Through the skilled motioning of his hands, Pastor artfully articulated what his tongue could not, as he expounded, saying, "Well let me tell you what perfect is. Perfect means, and is characterized by: a completion of a thing, to be full, being filled to the absolute top, spotless, entire, truthful, sincere, without blemish, upright, whole, a supply of something, to accomplish the task, being influential in a matter, the ending of something. It's a state of being, to make something, the expiration of a thing, which is substantially different from the end of a thing in substance, to finish as in doing all that could have been done till the time is up. Now do you understand what perfect is?"

"Now, I really don't know Pastor."

"You don't know what? Or is it that you don't know for sure if you want to be perfect or not, or to even give it a shot Deacon?"

"Now wait a minute Pastor, are you actually emphasizing that if a person is not perfect or all those things that you just named, he or she will not make it into the Kingdom of Heaven? Give me a straight yes or no!"

"No Deacon! I'm saying what I said at first. We are not perfect or doing the things that defines perfection, because we chose not to. In other-words,

The Perfect Lesson

we don't want to be perfect. Which makes it clear that we don't love God as we say we do."

"Oh my goodness..….No! No! No! No! Rev, don't say that. I know I love God. Can't any body tell me I don't love God. I don't care who it is. I know I love God and his son Jesus Christ. You gonna have to tell somebody else that. Speak for yourself on that one. Maybe you don't love him. But I know what he done for me. Early one Sunday morning: I said early one morning. Halleluiah! He died for me, and I accepted Jesus as my personal Lord and my risen Savior on one sanctified day. Oh no sirree! I know I love him. I can feel him in my heart right now. Glory! Thank ya' Jesus. He just put that in my spirit, Halleluiah! Halleluiah!"

Chapter 4
The Show down

The Deacon Board members began to nod their heads in agreement while swaying their bodies as if the spirit was moving them at that very moment with Deacon Zeek, and they all went, "Amen" except for Deacon Mark and Kenny. In a mild and quite manner the pastor asked, "So Deacons, are you keeping God's Word, and do what he says?"

None of the deacons spoke. It was quiet for a moment.

Then Zeek spoke out, "Well I try," he said in a happy-go-lucky sort of way.

The pastor folded his arm, looking straight in Zeek's eyes, and asked, "Do you always tell the truth and never tell lies Deacon Zeek?"

"For the most part, I always try to be honest and keep my word at all times with everyone," Zeek proudly responded.

Impatiently Gateway shot, "Stop the bull-shiten Deacon! Do you ever tell lies?"

"Do what?" Zeek replied somewhat startled. "Tell lies about what?"

Calmly Gateway walked closer to the Deacon till they were almost toe-to-toe. Now looking into Zeek's uncertain eyes, and requesting in a demanding and aggressive but controlled tone with spit jumping, "Do you keep God's word and do you always tell the truth and never tell lies to anyone? Think before you speak now."

Now What?

The assembled deacons all dressed in black suits, white shirt and black ties stood there with their heads bowed wondering what was going to happen next and what was Zeek going to say. It was like an 'OK Corral' Cow Boy Stand-off' scene, complete with loaded holsters, for Gateway and Zeek did have their Bible. Deacon Zeek paused and thought in a moment of silence, clenching his fist and rubbing his sweaty fingers together while looking over each of his shoulders, one at a time acknowledging the looks on the board member's faces and how they were standing behind him in a listening mode, especially noticing, Deacon Giz. Zeek began to breathe sigh-fully, inhaling and exhaling as if someone has caught up with him in a race, but time was running out, and the finish line just steps away. He began doubting if he was going to make it.

Now looking back into Gateway's eyes, and rubbing his nose, Zeek started to think about his own situation, but still not speaking a word. Calmly placing his hands in his pockets, drying them and

Young Darby

looking down at his shoes then lifted his head back up, and now his eyes met Gateway's penetrating eyes.

In a moment notice his thoughts carried him back about a few days ago when he was coming out of a corner store on his way home from the office.

He remembered this beautiful full figured ebony brown skinned woman, very big busted, with a slender waistline, hips measuring even with her shoulders. She was wearing a clinging skirt, cutting off barely below her thighs with every carving curb defined, and an exposing tightly fitting body blouse. She seemed to have been in pure voluptuous innocents as she approached him in need of local directions. Zeek always had a weakness and a strong attraction for fat butt, smooth legs, and big bosom women. Zeek recalled, as he watched her every curve in wantonness. He recalled fantasizing with her while his wife was on a church trip. He recalled as he gave her the directions in a fun, flirtatious and enjoyable manner in which he diverted in to small talk, with eyes trained on her bosom and legs most of the time, saying such things as, 'You sure do look gorgeous today honey. That skirt fits you like a glove.' And

The Perfect Lesson

'What's that stuff you're wearing smelling so good like that?' He remembered, tugging on his necktie saying, 'Your husband let you out like this a lot?' And the young lady, who could not have been more than 21, began blushing. Though not a member of his church, she heard him preach before but he didn't know it.

And Zeek said to her, 'I sure wouldn't mind treating you out one lovely evening with your fine tender self.'

Zeek snapped out of it and looked back at the pastor as if he was coming out of a light trance. But the pastor had done stepped back and was looking off again holding his right fist in his left hand with his back turned to Zeek while appearing to be in deep thought himself. Deacon Zeek thoughts returned back again to that evening while he was at home showering. For it was at this time that he thought of that woman that he saw that day with great intensity in an intimate way remembering lusting over every inch of her smooth soft silky flesh, and vanilla aroma, which he even smelt while he was standing there, even her lips held him captive. And when the thoughts of her filled his mind and heart, his imagination took control. When the name of Jesus came to him, his lustful enjoyment and thoughts of intimacy became dampened. But he deliberately, during those moments of intense lust, rejected all thoughts of Jesus and holiness until he completed his moments of indulging in his fantasyland.

When he was done with engaging himself with lustful gratification and fantasy, he returned to himself and the thoughts of Jesus and a heavy conviction came in like a flood-light beaming into a dark room, and he repented in his heart for blocking Jesus out and promised not to do it again even as he went to the bathroom and stood there washing his sinful hands.

Then as he stood there among the deacons and before Pastor Gateway, he thought to himself how many times that he has done this very samething and actually carried out the sins in the concealed arena of his mind whenever alone. Sometimes even in his mind, he let such imaginations roam and tarry with him in church meetings before their execution in one form or another. Then immediately his mouth opened and his jaws dropped, and he started nibbling on his thumbs and fingernails, and he lifted up his eyes, and this time, the pastor was looking at him.

Zeek's eyes meeting Gateway's eyes jolted him, and with reluctance, he began nodding his head slightly up and down admittingly, saying, "OK Pastor!" Then another pause, then, "Damn," he pouted, while skillfully kicking a rock from under a dirt mound and said, "You know Pastor, I really don't want to be perfect at times, 'it's true.

The Perfect Lesson

Well, I do and I don't. I must admit, I never really thought about it like this. But you know, the flesh is weak. I give you that! The Bible says that. But Now that you brought us out here to expound and magnify this matter, I'm gonna at least give this matter some deep consideration. I can see that it is a serious issue when you think about it."

Zeek then turned around to look at the other deacons, and Deacon Giz was looking at him with a stale look on his face.

Thinking Back

Then Zeek recalled last year when he and Deacon Giz stayed behind at church after communion and argued over the left-over wine, as to who was going to dispose of it. They flipped a coin but quickly reasoned among themselves that the coin could not decide who should drank it, because they were smarter than the coin, so they divided the wine, drunk it, became slightly twisted and reminisced on the other fun times, and how fine sister Shirley, Caroline and Judy butts were, especially Judy, and made jokes about the sizes of their butts.

They mostly joked about Judy who was extra big busted and whom Giz said her behind looked

Young Darby

like two basketballs shaking like jelly but her face look like, 'Mighty Joe Young'. They talked about how she always seems to be lonely and in need of counseling and often needed someone to talk to, and how they would like to satisfy her every need with more than talk. He recalled Giz saying, 'Man I'll rock her boat; house, car and world, just let her come to me for confession…. Hey! Who! Just put a bag over her head and her ass belong to me. Man you see how all the fine ones keep going to the Pastor?'

'Yeah!' Zeek said, feeling twisted, "No wonder he don't want us in there when he's so-called ministering to them. Shit, I wish he would let me minister to Shirley, man I'll be all night ministering to her. I'll minister to all of 'em: Marlene and Cora too. Man, she got it going on, Don't she?'

Giz said, 'Man, just give me that fat-ass sister Judy. Shoot man, I think I'm gonna go 'head and start a select group counseling ministry,' then he started rubbing his stomach, while chuckling about the whole thing.

'Well what'ya gonna do when they start swamping you with all those phone calls about their problems?' Giz started laughing out loud now, saying, 'Shi—t man, I aint the pastor, they start calling me too much, see what I do. Yo! No problem! I aint Gateway. I know how to work the Caller ID dud. Hey man, if I don't feel like being

The Perfect Lesson

bothered, shoot, especially late at night, you see this finger right here? I'll switch that 'bad boy' off so fast, it-uh make your head swim. I keep the speaker on though, so I could still hear whose calling at night, but if I'm tired I aint answering nothing. Hey, that's my time. No what um sayin' Big Brother? I tell'ya. Ma—-n, if I were the preacher, I wouldn't have any jive problems. I'll handle it. Man that's what the pastor should do sometimes. Let him keep on, he goin' be burnt out by next year. How much time you give 'em?'

And they sat there laughing about it like it was such a cool joke.

Chapter 5
He Saw Me

The Deacon held his head with both hands, messaging the temple region of his head with his fingers, and he turned back towards the pastor and continued, "You gonna have a hard time getting people to understand this."

"I know," the pastor said.

"It sure aint gonna be easy," Deacon Zeek added.

"Who you telling?" Pastor Gateway confirmed.

"You see, even I'm bucking against the prick. Honestly, it even flew over my head due to my own stubbornness and defensiveness, as if I knew I love God so much that I can't be questioned about it. And I know I don't do everything he say do. So maybe you're right, Jesus did say; you are my friends, *if* you do whatsoever I command you. In other words, you just can't be Jesus friend just by simply saying it. You have to do something to be his friend. You have to show it. Just like if you want to be my friend."

"That's what I'm talkin' about," said Gateway.

Zeek went on, "You have to keep God's word. And do all that he say do, because in a certain place in the Bible, he actually said, '*if* a man love me he

The Perfect Lesson

would keep my word'. And, 'he that doesn't love me doesn't keep my word'. And, 'if you keep my commandment you shall abide in my love'——- Then Jesus went on to say, *if you* love me *keep* my commandments.

Finally, he gave one of the most powerful reasons for us to do this, when he said, '*if a man keep my saying, he shall never see or taste of death'*.

You know pastor, sometime if one is not careful, one could easily believe that they know it all, especially when things seems to be going ok. The truth is, sometimes I feel like that."

"Like what?" the Pastor asked.

"Like I know it all. And a lot of times when I think that I'm right, I'm wrong. Yet still, even when I know what is clearly right, sometimes I push my responsibilities to do what is right, aside, into the recesses of my mind at times for convenience sake. And knowing this, and being honest right now at this moment, I also know that I don't keep his word all the time. But even though I'm not keeping his word, I insist that I love him anyway. Am I the only one doing this?" he asked as he looked around.

"Oh no Deacon, you have a lot of company!"

"But Pastor, can I really love him and not keep his word all the time?"

"I don't think so Deacon," answered Gateway, quipping with his robotic voice.

Young Darby

"Yeah, because Jesus says, if I don't keep his word I don't love him."

"Um hum," hummed the pastor.

Feeling convicted, Zeek turned around again and nodded in a confirming fashion to the assembled deacons and back at the pastor. The pastor marveled at his change in tone as well as his continence. Then Zeek said, "Excuse me Pastor, but we as people do what in the hell we want to do and say any damn thing we want to say out of our mouth.

It's like, we are some kind of gods or something ourselves with the power of life and death in our very own hands with no one to answer to or give an account to. And its like, we can do anything without him seeing or knowing.

I know this don't sound good, but I'm sure the Lord have proof that I don't love him like I say I do, especially when I call myself praying so fervently, because *if* I really love him, I *would* keep his whole word, after the praying is done regardless of temptation. I would keep his total word, not partly keeping his word. I *would* be perfect even as my Father in heaven is perfect to the best of my ability, like you are saying. If not completely perfect, I would at least be honest, because he simply told me to be perfect. But if I say, 'no I cant', or 'this is not what he really means', I'*m then* being disobedient, and show that I don't love him as I ought to, or even as I say that I do, regardless of what I want

The Perfect Lesson

to believe or want people to believe about me. Because what it all comes down to is what God knows and says about me and he's gonna keep his word anyway, about what he said he's gonna do!

Chapter 6
"I Can Do All Things…"

"So Pastor, I think we better start showing that we love him by keeping His Word and doing His will. And not just by flapping our 'traps'. This is the only true way we can say that we love 'em, and that we are Christians. Truthfully Pastor, Deacons, God the Father, Jesus Christ, and all who are listening, I have a confession to make before you all. I aint shit, and I'm not fit for the Kingdom. The truth is, I'm a deceiver, and not a 'For-real for-real' Christian. But as of this very moment, I declare to you all, that I renounce all sin, and purpose whole-heartedly in my heart to follow in Jesus footsteps, and to be a Christian. And now Pastor, I got to go."

"Where ya' goin' Deacon."

"I'm gonna go and have a little talk with the Lord in private..... No! A big talk with the Lord. I believe you're right Pastor."

"You do huh?"

"Yeah! It's praying time for me. I just don't think the Lord would tell me to do something knowing that I can't do it or that he would not help me to do."

With glistening eyes of passion, Deacon Zeek lifted his voice saying, "Pastor, I don't care what

The Perfect Lesson

any damn devil, demon, people or thing may say, think, proclaim or insinuate: now that I think of it, I believe it's true.

I don't know how long its gonna take me, but I believe that I can be perfect, because the Bible said that I can do all things through Christ who strengthens me. And the Word said, 'Greater is he that is in me than he that is the world'. And that, I am 'more than a conqueror…' I must be perfect even as my Father in heaven is perfect. Perfect in that, I will keep his word. I must do all that Jesus say do. All that I know to do, I must do. And I will do it so help me God. In the Name Of Jesus."

Kneeling on both knees, the Deacon began praying in other tongues as the spirit gave him utterances, but Deacon Giz showed stubborn resistance still, as he stood there frowning with fidgeting hands.

"Amen. That's all I can say brother Deacon. Amen," Gateway said proudly looking on Zeek.

"I got to get a few things straight in my life. I'm glad we had this meeting Pastor. Now I'm gonna find out, all that God really want me to do, and if I'm doing all that I know right now, point-blank."

"You don't know if you're doing all God want you to do Deacon?" Gateway asked.

"No! Let me stop faking even right now. I know I'm not doing all that I know to do right now pastor. You know, If I where to block out the way I see things, and judge my current lifestyle by the Bible, the Bible would show that I don't love God and that I love the world and is a friend of this old world with severely strong ties. I must change."

"Halleluiah," shouted Gateway.

Now all the deacons seemed to be thinking and nodding their heads.

Zeek continued, "What am I gonna do when I see Jesus face to face?

I can't see myself trying to explain that I didn't think he really meant it, when He said, 'B*e ye perfect.....*' or 'Keep my word if you love me.'"

Zeek turned around and looked at the other deacons and said, "To me now, to be perfect, and to keep his word, is to love God. I've been missing the mark fellez."

"I'm with you brother," said Mark.

"Me too dude," said Kenney.

Giz now biting his fingers, walked up to Zeek and said, "So how you figure on being perfect?"

"The way I figure Deacon Giz, if I keep his word, I would be without a fault. And if I were without fault, I would be without spot or blemish, perfect even as the Father in heaven is perfect or at least as he called me to be. My flesh and some gravity of my thoughts might not be perfectly matured, but I will be perfect in my present moments, and this is good to understand. Then, when I see Jesus I could hold my head up and look at him even as he looks

The Perfect Lesson

at me. Oh what a wonderful day that would be, and what cleanness! Or, even if I would just be honest with no deceit in me, that would be a start. Oh my goodness! What freshness of being! What joy, even if not perfect but totally and lovingly honest with God's word. Like the pastor said: that must count for something."

"So you really think that you could be perfect, huh Deacon Zeek?" Deacon Giz insisted.

"Well hey! Why not? Who should I believe is right? God saying I don't love him because I don't keep his word, or me saying I do love him, even if I don't keep his word all the time because I keep it sometimes and count it as keeping his word all the time or enough?"

Gateway pet his hand like he was clapping for Deacon Zeek, walked up to him and they hugged as if understanding a new emerging revelation.

After standing face to face looking at each other for a minute or so, slowly the two leaned forward until their heads touched and their eyes welled, till watered, and a stream of tears ran from the pastor's eyes first. And Deacon Zeek could not hold back an inner groaning that bubbled out, "Ahhh, Huh!" Then his tears rolled down his cheeks and over his slightly trembling lips. They hugged again and embraced each other in what seemed to have been a 'meeting of the minds' and discovery, but they could not speak for their throats were full of emotions that they could not readily swallow.

The assembled deacons fell to their knees and began praying with their natural minds and some in other tongues. Deacon Giz still showed reluctance even though he had kneeled and gotten into a praying posture.

Suddenly a mighty cool wind blew upon them all. The Pastor and Zeek sobbed with a louder groaning seemingly coming from their bellies.

They began secretly hiding their tears from one another while privately drying their face with their shirtsleeves and shirttails. And most of the Deacons seemed to have been caught up in prayer, but Deacon Giz seemed a little disgusted as he checked his watch for the time and kept looking around like he had to go somewhere.

In silence, Zeek and the Pastor shook hands, looking in each other's eyes with a lingering firm and gripping handshake.

Zeek slowly retrieved his hands ever so purposefully, planted them in his pockets, nodding his head at the well-dressed assembly of deacons and at the pastor as he slowly backwardly walked a way.

'The righteousness of the perfect shall direct his way..'

Prov. 11:5

The Perfect Lesson

The Pastor stood there for a while looking on at the Deacon as he walked away, admiring the dedication he discovered in Deacon Zeek.

With both feet glued to the ground and with weighted legs, Gateway noticed that he still could not move his feet, nor did he try very hard. He also seemed to have found something igniting in himself as well, but he just couldn't move or didn't want to move. He even looked down repeatedly at his feet in awe, wondering why he could not move his feet, but without a hint of panic. He even smiled at the resistance when he tried to move as if he began to enjoy that he could not move during these moments. After a closing prayer he dismissed the assembled deacon, but he remained standing there for a short while afterwards.

Part Two
No More Bull Baby

The Deacon arrived home late that evening with a glow about him that even Ellen haven't seen, and a hint of eager determination that made him look like he was intensely thinking about something that should be shared. When he entered his house, his wife, Ellen greeted him and he grabbed her and firmly planted a kiss onto her plush soft cheeks. Cornering his demeanor within her stare, she curiously asked, "Well, what's up Deak? You sure look fired-up about somethin'. Mind sharing?"

"What's for dinner, Honey? I'm hungry," Zeek said as he went straight to the refrigerator with eyes searching every corner of the 'box' for a quick bite, as if he did not hear her.

"Ooooh! Just sat down I'm coming. Here, drink this nice cold glass of water it'll refresh you while I get your supper."

"Thanks dear," he said as he received the glass of spring water while walking to the dinning table to pull up a chair.

Eager to find out why her husband, was looking so different, Ellen came rather hastily with his meal. She set it before him, waited until he blessed

The Perfect Lesson

it then continued, "Sweety, are you ready to tell me what's going on?"

"Sweet heart, nothing but the truth 'so help' me. The Reverend Gateway and I had a real talk today.

I mean a real talk. And to make a long story short, the Reverend Gateway and myself, is gonna stop 'bull-shiten'."

"What?" Ellen exclaimed, holding one hand over her mouth and half standing up from her chair. "What do you mean by that? I'm confused," she said, looking as if she was at a lost for words, scratching her head, then placing both hands on her waist as if to say, 'This better be good!' Ellen's mouth remained opened, but no words came out.

Zeek went on, "Ella-honey, we decided that we are gonna start preaching, teaching, and walking the whole, total truth. No more lies. No more of that wishy-washy, make ya' feel good stuff and prosperity right now for everybody stuff, name it, believe it, you got it stuff. Well sometimes ya' may still feel good, and prosper here and there, but it will be the truth doing it to you."

With much anticipation, Ellen asked, bringing her hand back over her mouth again, "Well, what have y'all been lying about, excuse me, 'bull-shiting' about?"

"No. You don't understand honey."

"Understand what? All of this time I thought that y'all been teaching, preaching, and walking the truth the best you knew how. Now you're gonna just waltz in here and tell me that y'all was just bull-shitin'?"

"No! Sweet heart, it's like this. We have been doing part of the works and most of that was the part that you could see, but when it came down to it, in our own personal life and belief system, we did not believe the real issue that the Lord put before us."

"And what issue is that?"

"The Lord said if you love me, keep my word. Not some times.

Not most of the time or when you are serving in the office for the Lord, or when you are being seen before men, or while you are at the church house, but he said, keep my word period. Always. And now we believe the Lord meant it when he said, we should be perfect even as the Father in heaven is perfect. We don't take the word perfect likely no more. We believe that he really meant it, besides, the word of God is full of too much proofs and evidence for us to go on believing that it's not true."

"So you mean to tell me that you and pastor are gonna be out there telling people that they suppose to be perfect like God?"

"Yes Maim!"

Ellen quietly laughed while shaking her head saying, "Oh my goodness. There goes the church. Have you thought about this?"

The Perfect Lesson

"Yes Maim, but I know what you thinking baby! But It's gonna be alright because even if we don't be perfect, no one can say we didn't believe it or try to do God's word."

Looking strangely at her husband with her head slightly tilted to the left, she said, "And what do you mean by that?"

"Well for starters, before today, I never thought Jesus wanted us or anyone to be perfect, but now I know he does. I can feel it in my heart. So even if I'm not perfect right now, I can start to become perfect. All it takes is me doing all that I know is right. If I do all that I know is right before God all the time, one day I will walk before him perfectly, It's that simple.

The questions is, am I ready to do all that I know is right. That is the question for everyone."

"Tell me something, Zeek', didn't you read this in the Bible before?"

"Yes I did, my dear, but I told you, I never accepted it."

"Well what took you so long to accept it?"

"I don't know. All I can say is, I wasn't really ready to accept it back then, and besides, I really wasn't trying to be perfect. Plus I was taught that you really didn't have to be perfect and the Bible was speaking figuratively about perfection. Just do the best you can and you would still go to heaven. Boy, wasn't I the jerk?"

Young Darby

"Yes! I guess you was."

"What you mean by that?"

"No comment," Ellen teased, as she went back to the kitchen.

"As if you already knew", Zeek casually remarked.

"The truth is, my dear husband, I already knew that that was what Jesus said, as well as what he meant. I guess we can say that I was just trying to be the obedient, and submissive wife. And besides, I was becoming somewhat convinced that we, being only human, were not really instructed to be perfect.

I never heard a sermon exclusively on it and no one that I knew ever talked about it. Nothing is said about it or commanded about it in our church nor, have I heard any details and reference to this teaching in any other church, on the TV or from the radio. ———But you know! About a year ago I remember reading that scripture in Matthews 5th chapter one time and meditating on it, and shortly afterwards that day, I saw an incredible vision, in which a huge vehicle ran over a patch of grass.

At first I didn't see the blades of grass because of the clouds of dust, debris and soiling from previous vehicle barreling down on the ground. Later on, as certain drivers pulled their vehicle off the road and considered the impacted area, I saw one of the drivers point out to the little kid that was

The Perfect Lesson

with him, that there were still roots in the ground in the heavily traveled area. Another driver who was already parked along the roadside over-heard the first driver. So after they together observed the spotted patch, they agreed that it was so.

Then a small boy came over to me while I was in this trance, if that's what I can call it, and said, 'Let enough serious drivers continue to travel this road, I bet you, eventually more of them would consider the roots of one of the faint lingering live strains of grass, but your average driver may never notice it. The fate of the roots of that grass is another story.' Like you and the Pastor discovered the meaning of Mt 5:48 in which many overlooked, so did I. But I'm glad you are doing something with your revelation, because I was kind of lost with mines. Now that we look back, we can see that this truth that you found was there all the time. Huh! Just because you don't see it don't mean it isn't there."

"You know dear, you have a point there. I'm just glad the Lord allowed me to give heed to his word. But man, this is a heavy part of his word. This might be the most important part of his word. But hold it!" Zeek exclaimed with both hands on his waist: "Why you never told me about this vision of yours before?"

"I don't know!"

Young Darby

Knock! Knock! Knock!

"I got it," said Zeek as he shuffled to the front door.

"Who is it?" he asked, while straining to peep thru the peephole with one eye. He could only see the back of the person's head, for whoever it was had his or her back facing the door and would not readily answer.

"Who is it dear?" Ellen curiously asked.

Knock! Knock! Knock!

The knocking this time was slightly harder, louder, urgent and quicker in successions. Zeek hurried-up and peeped thru the peephole again, but again the person had turned their back to the door. Zeek briskly but quietly turned to his wife and whispered, "They wont say anything, and his back is still turned, and by it being dark out, I can't see his face."

"Why they wont speak?" anxiously asked, Ellen.

"I don't know! He's just standing there with his back to the door."

"Maybe he's casing our neighborhood. I'm gonna call the police."

"No baby."

The Perfect Lesson

"You just stay right there. Don't take your eyes off of him. OK?"

"But hold it baby. Wait' a minute! What ya' gonna report? That someone is knocking on the door?" Zeek asked, fighting to keep his voice down while trying feverishly to make a point.

"Well, what you gonna do?"

"Shoosh…shoosh…shoosh…"

"Don't sh-sh-sh me, you just can't stand there peeping at him all night. Let's call, 911 and report it as suspicious behavior then."

"Hold it sweetheart! Just a' minute! I'm just gonna open the door and see what he want. Hand me that bat right over there in the corner," Zeek said while pointing at the bat.

"Wait' a minute, suppose he have some kind of weapon?"

"A weapon?"

"Yeah! Suppose he have a gun?"

"Just give me that bat right quick."

"Don't you think this is strange?" Ellen asked as she nervously handed him the baseball bat.

"Don't worry baby, this aint that kind of neighborhood," Zeek said, as he situated the baseball bat with a rock solid grip so that it would be out of sight when he opened the door, but just behind the door with his fingers clutching the top neck of the bat.

Looking slightly frighten, Ellen asked, "If everything is OK, why are you holding the bat like that?"

"Just in case."

"But what are you gonna do?"

"Just go back in there baby, I got this," Zeek said while waving and signaling her to go to the kitchen.

Ellen gasping with shallow breaths and holding her hands together like she were praying, reluctantly went back into the kitchen area.

Gateway's Prayer

In the mean while, the pastor was back at the temple in front of the altar in fervent prayer: My Father who art in Heaven, help me to be a better treasure. I'm tired of going along with these games, give me a chance to make a change. Teach me to do a work for you. And make me an arrow in your string, aim me at the heart of things. Make me to stand for what is true, keep me from acting like a fool. Don't want to be a fool any more, that's why I'm pleading on this floor. Help me to preach not for money, but I need that money, aint tryin' to be funny. The deacon say they frown at giving,

The Perfect Lesson

but how am I supposed to make a living? When I even buy a new tie, your people give me looks of, 'Why'? Every time I buy a suit, they say the pastor think he's cute. When I pleaded for a new car, they said that damn preacher gone too far. When I desired that cruising trip, most board members button-up their lips. Oh' Lord Help me to keep my zeal, 'cause if looks could kill, I'd be dead for real. Help me to try to understand the complications in the heart of man. The sour looks they fight to hide really show when I preach on tithes. O' why O' why when it's time to tithe: O' my O' my they make me cry: O' why O' why when it's time to tithe, O' my O' my I want to hide. They make me want to run and hide when it's time for them to pay that tithe. Some even say I need a job, like pastoring your flock is not so hard. I know you heard all these bells I rang, but sometime I got to tell you everything. Thank you for listing to all my chatter now teach me to do what really matters. I'm saying this prayer locked in this pose in this hole tryin' hard not to let go. Nevertheless, while going thru this test, I'm trying my best not to slip in this mess, but I do truly confess I'm growing weary from this test. To change some things I call your name, save me from these vicious endless games. Oh' Lord, this pit is mighty strange, but when I come out I'll shout your Holy name. Your holy name is everything: O' lord my God please make it plan. Please make it plan,

Young Darby

in Jesus name. In Jesus name I say it again, please make it plan in Jesus name. Um listening Lord, Amen.

As was his routine, Pastor Gateway got up off of his knees, wiped his eyes with his worn out hanky, and left the church.

Back At The Deacon's House

As the tension mounted, Deacon Zeek continued to assess the situation by trying desperately to peep out the peephole to catch a glimpse of the stranger's face, by calling out, shouting, knocking on the door himself, and demanding thru the door that the stranger state their business. Again Zeek shouted, "Who is it got-dam-it?" But now, the man was rocking back and forward on his heels with his back still turned towards the door. Zeek took a big deep breath, grabbed the bat and snatched the door open, cocked his wrist back, while holding the bat behind him in his right hand with a rock solid grip, "Do you have a hearing problem Mr.?" Zeek exploded as the door flung opened.

The stranger slowly turned around, and muttered in stammering broken speech, "Are you the De De De De Deacon Z Z Z Zeek, of The New Church Of Z Z Z Zion on Sa Sa Sa Saint Matthew Street also called Ssssaint Mmmathews?"

The Perfect Lesson

"Who is it honey?" frantically, Ellen yelled out from the kitchen. Dropping the bat behind the door, looking confused, with his voice now lowered, Zeek said, "I believe it's one of the new members, Honey." With a sigh of relief, but filled with curiosity, he answered the man, "Yes! I'm he. What can I do for you tonight, and what's your name?"

Stammering he said, "I'm Steve Wi, Wi, Wilton. I wa, wa was tttt-old if you pray for me, my stamm.... stamm. stam... I was told that my, my, my,my my, ttttttalk would bbbbbe OK and mmmmy hhhhhee.. hearing would bbbbe OK ttttto."

"Come in, sir," Zeek said while turning around at a lost of words, looking for his wife to say something. For by this time she was edging her way back into the living room and was now in good hearing distance of the visitor, but she only looked at Zeek with her mouth open. Dropping her head as she fully reentered the living room, she sat down and kindly exchanged greetings with the visitor, Steve. There was a brief moment of silence.

Zeek broke the silence: "Well Steve, exactly who sent you here?"

"I didn't get the name, bbbbbut she said you wwa wa wa was a rightious ma ma ma ma man and some of the other mem, mem, members agreed while they was talkin' and said your name

Young Darby

annnnd clclclclclaim you gggget what eeeever you wwwant, bebebecause you're man of GGGod."

Zeek set down, bowed and shook his head, rubbing the back of his neck.

Suppose He Don't Get Healed!

Ellen caught Steve's eye and said, "Let me get you something to drink, Steve."

"Th-Thank you," said Steve.

Ellen got up and went to the kitchen, then called, "Oh Zeek! Can I see you for a moment please?"

"Excuse me one moment Steve," Zeek said as he made way to the kitchen. But Steve was looking down when Zeek said this and said nothing in reply. In the kitchen, Ellen asked Zeek, "What you gonna do?"

"I don't know baby, I guess I'll just read a scripture with him or two."

"Why did somebody send him to our home without any notice or at least a phone call or somethin'?"

"I don't know baby! And you see how he keeps starring at me while I was talking? I think something is really wrong with him."

"Honey that's because he can't hear," Ellen explained.

"What?"

"He can't hear."

The Perfect Lesson

"How you know?"

"He said that you could make his hearing OK! Say something to him from in here to see if he can hear you."

"Yeah, right!"

"No! I'm serious, Go ahead: ask him something!"

"Like what?"

"Call his name, see if he will respond, but don't let him see your face."

"Why he can't see my face?"

"Because, he will be able to read your lips—-Duh!"

"What?"

"Go ahead now Honey, it's getting late."

"But suppose he can hear?"

"Then that's all good too, but I doubt it."

"But suppose he can't hear at all, baby?"

"Then pray for him Deacon!"

"Yeah! I know. I don't mind praying, but the way they sent him over here, he might think he's gonna get healed right away."

"Well suppose he do?"

"But suppose he don't, he's gonna think it don't work."

"He's gonna think what don't work?" Ellen asked with both hands on her hips as if she was growing inpatient.

"You know what I mean, baby!"

"Deacon Ezekiel Jedthow Robinson!"

Young Darby

"But Sweet Heart?"

"Zeek, are you concerned about him getting healed right after you pray for him?"

The Deacon slowly inhaled, leaned forward and shook his head, as if he was defeated, looked up heavenward and said, "Why Lord? Do you want me to pray for this man? Will you heal him now? Tonight Lord? In the name of Jesus?"

"Zeek, first at least go on in there and shout out somethin' while he's not looking, to see if he can hear you."

"I can do that from here baby."

"Well do it then, 'Mr. Newly-Not-Taking-Any-More-Bullshit Perfect Man'." Zeek looked at his wife with his mouth open and fixated for a moment. Now with an attitude of no more tolerance he did not care what happened next, looking on at Steve, though Steve head was turned towards the TV, Zeek shouted at the top of his lungs, "Hey Steve! Can you hear me now?"

Being off guard, Ellen jumped, and to his amazement, Steve swung around with his mouth wide open and began to cry tears of joy, saying, "Thank you Deacon. May God bless you!

Thank you for praying for me. Halleluiah Jesus! Glory to the Most High God who has sat the universe in order and who have perfected praise in babes. Who raised the dead, healed the sick, fed the hungry, gave sight to the blind, healed the lame

The Perfect Lesson

and gave his life on Calvary that I might live to receive my hearing and correctness of speech on this marvelous day. May only blessing come on this house now and forever. Oh thank you brother Deacon. It's all true, all that they said about you."

The Deacon looked at Ellen and said, "Look! He's not stumbling anymore". Ellen fainted on the kitchen floor. Steve stood at the door praising God. He even prayed to God in other tongues as he thanked God for sending him to the Deacon. Zeek went over to Steve to shake his hand, but Steve grabbed and bear-hugged the Deacon with a snug bear hug while profusely sobbing and crying.

Shortly afterwards, Ellen slowly got up off the kitchen floor and leaned on the oven looking out at Steve and the Deacon not knowing what to say. Steve and Zeek shook hands, exchanged a few farewells and Zeek opened the door and Steve left praising God.

With tightly zipped lips and eyes of fire, Zeek eyes searched the walls and the ceilings for an answer, but did not say a word. He and Ellen remained silent all thru that night with great amazement and wonder.

Young Darby

Chapter 7
She Caught Me!

It was another Sun-crisp morning and the phone almost ranged off the hook before Ellen answered it.

"Hello. The Robinson's"

"Hi Ella! Thank God for your husband, he did it again. We told Steve he could do it. We told 'em. Halleluiah. Praise him."

Ellen paused, then asked, "Is this Shirley?"

"Oh! I'm sorry baby. Yes! It's me. How is the Deacon?"

"He's doing fine. What Time is it?"

"11:30."

"What? Let me get the Deacon up. We went to bed a little late last night. But Shirley, um what did you mean by, '…he did it again'?"

"Well, don't you remember when Bent Mike came to your place last month?" Ellen looked dumbfounded, (Only if Shirley could see her face) and asked, "Yeah! What about it?"

"Well, he said Deacon Zeek shouted out to him something about his condition, and the next thing he knew, his back started to tingle and by the time he reached his house he was walking as straight as an arrow with no pain whatsoever and didn't have to get that surgery he was schedule for the next day.

The Perfect Lesson

Girl you didn't here his testimony in church that following Sunday?"

"Well no, we thought he kept his appointment the next day. That's all he talked about at the house: how promising he thought the surgery would be."

"So you mean to tell me you didn't know the Deacon did it."

"Shirley, the Deacon didn't heal Bent Mike!"

"Well God did it thru the Deacon!"

"Now that sounds better. And I'm so glad Steve is well now too. And please give everyone our love."

"Ok, dear."

"See you Sunday."

"OK baby."

Ellen felt a little lightheaded and anxious as she began shoving Zeek.

"Zeek...Zeek. Wake up!"

"Hu.. Huh.. Hum?"

"You're becomin' a little popular these days."

"What baby?"

"It's after 11 o'clock in the morning, and guess who I just hung-up from talkin' with?"

Zeek put on his guessing game face; "Uhm, Steve?"

"No"

"Oh boy! Uhm! The Pastor?"

"No!"

"Deacon Giz?"

Young Darby

"Try again."

He thought about her referring to him as being popular and for some reason, Shirley came to his mind but he didn't want to guess her name so said, "Ok! I give, who was it?"

"Shirley!"

"Sister Shirley?"

"Yep."

"His eyes bulged opened as he asked, "What did she want?"

Ellen casually climbed off the bed and strolled to the middle of the bedroom floor as if she was taking the center stage with an all knowing smirk on her face, twirling a string of lace back and forth about her wrist, squinting her eyes and nodding her head as if she knew a secret.

Now, with eyes wide-open and fully awaken, Zeek asked; "What did she say? I mean what did she want? I mean…."

"She said that she was one of them who referred Steve here for his healing."

"Oh yeah?"

"But that's not all. Wait until you hear this. I think you better hold on to your seat cause I just don't know how you going to react to this."

"Oh boy! What is it now?"

"I mean I am blown away. I don't know if I should believe it or not," Ellen said, now looking a bit serious, as if in deep thought about her husband.

The Perfect Lesson

"What Dear? What else?

"Now, how should I put it?"

"Come on, just tell me what she said. Is it really that hard?"

"Are you ready?

"Yeah baby, I'm ready. Why all the suspense?"

"Cause I'm not even ready for this, and if you think last night was something...."

"Oh come-on baby. What did she say?"

"She said…"

"Hold it! You don't have to tell me, I think I know!"

"What was it then?"

"Steve was faking wasn't he? I knew it. I knew it. I knew it."

"No sweet heart he wasn't faking?"

"Then what's-up with all the suspense?"

"Ok! Ok," Ellen said shaking her head in disbelief and taking a chair, looking at her baffled husband.

Then all of a sudden Zeek's face changed, for he knew in his heart what it was.

In his mind, he flashed back to the time when he and Deacon Giz drank and fantasized of Shirley big breast and fat butt and how he wanted to do it to her, and a cloud of conviction came over him

Young Darby

for he thought that maybe for some reason Deacon Giz told on him, because Giz heard him say he was going to try to be perfect and teach a more excellent word, and Giz was an 'old schooler'. Not the type that's very quick to forgive. Not the type to take to too many new Ideas and approaches, specially of somebody trying to be perfect or attempting to persuade others to that capacity to achieve perfection. Oh no! Giz would not have this. Giz would rather climb Mount Everest instead, Zeek thought.

Zeek looked at Ellen, as guilt streamlined his face with eyes unable to meet Ellen's. "Ella Oh Ella do you still love me?"

"Oh my goodness, I'm sorry dear it's just that its all just happen so suddenly, specially with what happen last night, now all of a sudden, "Shirley calling and telling me...."

"No Darling. No that's OK you don't have to say it if you don't want too. I believe I understand."

"But let me finish..."

"But Sweety!"

"No, no, no. Let me tell you now. It's just so hard for me and I know this might even be harder for you, but maybe something is on your life that

The Perfect Lesson

you don't know about. Maybe the Lord is really trying to use you."

Zeek confidently perked up, but cautiously sat on the edge of the bed and said ever so patiently; "Ella my dear, what did Shirley say?"

"She said that last month you healed, Bent Mike."

The Deacon leaped off the bed shrieking, "Holy Lord! What? Who? Me? What? What's wrong with that lady?"

"Well…"

"Is she crazy?"

The Deacon began briskly pacing back and forth from the Dresser to the bed as Ellen pulled out his most comfortable brown well creased cotton trousers, his matching cotton nylon shirt, and cap which covers only the top portion of his head as the typical Islamic type cap or the Jewish head piece. For one would rather push an elephant thru a door rather then try to make him wear something else.

Zeek was only about five feet 5' 6 inches but compactly built. Deacon Giz often compared Zeek strength to the Biblical Samson, and teased him when he wore his Kufi, saying that he wore it to hide his bald spot. He also teased him about keeping his hair cut close to hide his bald spot as well.

Young Darby

As Zeek wasted no time dressing, Ellen stood in the doorway waiting to hear what he would say in his obvious moments of surprise. "Honey, I'm off to this day's race please pray for me, because I don't know what this all mean or what it's going to lead to."

"Don't worry, you know the Lord knows what he's doing."

"Yes, but it would help me a little better I think, If he would clue me in a bit more. And how in the world do they figure that I had anything to do with these healings? Is it because it happened in our home?"

Then in a moment his eyes opened wide and he became instantly excited as if he just received and epiphany, saying, "Hey, maybe our house has a special anointing on it so that people who needs to be healed only have to come over."

"Sweetheart, I know you don't even believe that yourself."

Well baby something's goin'–on and I'm gonna find out. I'm gonna talk with the Pastor. Maybe he can shine some light on this matter a little bit."

"You think he would know the answer Zeek?"

"I don't know baby, but maybe he can give me some kind of explanation."

"But I thought you said you was gonna talk with Jesus? I aint trying to take anything away from the Pastor, but you know that Jesus knows!——-Right?"

The Perfect Lesson

"I know Dear," he said as he caressed Ellen's soft slender five-foot sleek frame with his strong arms and planted his lips into her plush cheeks as she kissed in the wind. I'll call you when I get settled Sweety," he said as he shaped his kufi and took off.

Pastor Gateway was in a consultation with one of the church senior members who often came by with many problems and with things that she thought would be a problem, and also relating to things in and out of the church that she thought the Pastor should know or do something about or preach against.

".... So Pastor, I just want you to know I really think it's a shame how sister Joe Linda is still shacking up. You see how she has been falling out in church, and everytime you touch her in the praying line she falls down and be wobbling and sprawling all across the floor like that? It's kind'a hard to imagine, aint it?"

"Well Sister Betty how do you know she's...."

"Just believe me, I know! Why ya' think she keeps goin' to the Single's Retreat?"

"I would say, for spiritual enrichment. She is a Christian, you know!"

Young Darby

"Ump! Spiritual enrichment my toe. She's been retreating. And I mean, Reeeee-Treeea—ting every Tom, Harry and Dick."

"Sister Betty," Gateway exclaimed, covering his mouth, as if he was embarrassed. Apparently nervous he cleared his voice, stroking his thinly laid jet-black mustache and seemed to have been in deep thought. He then arose from his chair and extended his hands towards Betty for prayer.

"Sister Betty let's pray that the Lord will strengthen Sister Joe Linda and cover her with his grace and mercy..."

"I wish I head time, but Pastor I got to go now. But you go ahead and pray for her though.

She need all the prayers she can get, and if I don't forget, I will pray for her tonight myself."

Then she mumbled under her breath, as she approached the door, "Don't know what good prayin' for that fool gonna do!"

When she left, the pastor went over and closed his office door and began to pray for Sister Betty's peace and joy and begged that God would touch and fill her with his presents:

"Oh Dear Father, we need for you to stop by here today Lord. We are all in a heap of a mess down here and Satin's smoke screen of deception is fogging up our vision so we can't see clearly. Wake us up Lord to righteousness. Remove the fog. Speak to us Lord. Pour out your Holy Spirit today on this place.

The Perfect Lesson

Anoint my office with a double portion. Remove the unclean thing from sister Betty. Blow upon her head the cool and gentle winds of contentment. Shadow her with your presents. Destroy her yoke. Remove the beam from her eye Oh Lord. Heal and deliver her right now Oh Lord Jesus!"

Gateway began to clinch his fists and raised his voice, bolden his stance, and switched into high gears, declaring, In your disgust lose not your trust but please loose grace and mercy on us. Why ya' makin' us get ready, don't forget our sister, Betty: sort of hurt by a flirt that wore a quiet familiar skirt. Help her Lord to understand you are the God with Master Plans. She's' been brooding with mouth moving with much affection in wrong direction. Before you drop that awesome ceiling, please pour out a mighty healing, to give us chance to turn around, before we all end up-side-down. I come too far not to see your face, that's why I need amazing grace. Lord forgive me for all my sins: at first I thought they'll make me win but now I know without a doubt my sins and friends will take me out. In your disgust don't count me out, um gonna fight and make my mark and carry cross to win your house. Um coming home to be with you when my call right here is through. Down here I ate so much dust, for the games I played was dangerous. I thank you lord for teaching me, to keep my eyes on

Young Darby

you and see, and when I'm thru at the end, I'll get that crown, for that's when real life begins, Amen.

He prayed the last part of his prayer from the top of his voice. Though church workers outside of his office that passed by heard him praying thru the door, they dared not comment to one another, as it seemed that they were use to hearing the pastor praying out loud from time to time in his office in this manner. But a certain worker by the name of Delores always stopped what she was doing and sat or stood completely still whenever she would hear him pray and seemed to relish in agreement on every word until he finished and afterwards be refreshed, but the pastor would never notice her doing this, for she was a faithful and quiet spirit of the church who never received nor wanted any praise, certificates or attention for the work that she was doing for the church. And it would be impossible to find her during recognition ceremonies. Nor would she attend such occasions, for she desired that Jesus would be her only reward for work done in this life. Most of the time she was looked over anyway, because she never spoke up for her rights as others. She wore long garments, plain colored blouses, no jewelry, or make-up, but she did wear hair ware and hair ties, and was very humble and soft-spoken. Mostly she would only speak to the children whom she taught at the morning service. She was also on the usher board and missionary team.

The Perfect Lesson

Some of the missionaries at the church, as well as from other neighboring or branch churches did not particularly like Delores because she seemed too content.

Even though she was without a husband or man friend, she was content, and nor did she seemed to desire one or ever spoke of any. She also shied away from conversation that involved dating so much so that some said that she was gay. A few of the church workers who observed her today, sneered at Delores while watching her from behind as she stood completely still with one hand on the wall in the hallway, about 15 meters down from the pastor office while he yet prayed.

Knock knock knock!

"Come in."

Zeek humbly entered Gateway's office with a puzzled look on his face.

"Hey! Hi you doing Buddy," the pastor greeted.

"I don't know Pastor."

"You mind sharing with me?" the Pastor replied with his Jet-black heavy eyebrows seemingly about to jump off his face, as he squinted his eyes in anticipation as he acknowledged Zeek's puzzled look.

Young Darby

"Well first of all Pastor for this encounter can I call you Doc? Cause I need a quick diagnoses."

"If it helps, go ahead."

Zeek told Gateway about the two incidents and the resulting healings and how perplexed he was that both healings happened without his direct knowledge.

"So you see Doc, the thing that bother me the most is that they both happened without my knowledge, even in my own house. How can this be?"

The Pastor began to rub his cleanly shaven chin and stroking his mustache as in deep thought. He paused for a few seconds before speaking and Zeek sat there on the edge of his seat leaning so far forward as though he did not need the chair. The Pastor put both hands on his desk and asked, "The Lord hasn't answered you yet, huh?"

"No sir."

The Pastor bowed his head with both hands on the top back part of his head while rubbing it as if trying to come up with an answer. There was silence again for about another minute or two. "Let's pray Deacon!"

Deacon Zeek stretched forth both of his hands across the desk. They joined hands and the Pastor began, "Lord you said where there are two or more together in your name...."

And they both began to pray in the spirit as the spirit gave utterance. They prayed this way for about thirty minutes without observing the time. When they finished they were both standing in separate corners in the office not knowing at what point they released each other's hands.

"Thank you pastor, for it was given to me that the answer to my concerns is not in words, but in being. And in by and by."

"In being? In by and by?" the pastor questioned, stroking his lips with his thumb.

"Yeah—- I don't understand it either," Zeek replied.

Looking very calm and full of peace, the pastor said, "Well go with peace anyway my good man: be strong, and always acknowledge the joy of the Lord.

And call me later this evening, I want you in the line up this Sunday to give a word."

"Will do Pastor!"

My Secret Condition

As Zeek left, he thought that he would look for some new food for thought since he would be ministering the word this coming Sunday, so he went next door to the church's bookstore and began searching, looking for a book that would just leap off the shelf at him. With great expectation

Young Darby

he searched the shelves. He looked around for about 45 minutes, but to his surprise, couldn't find anything that would leap out at him, so decided that he would just pray and read the word and use his Strong's Concordance for in-depth meaning and examination of the word. As he was about to leave the bookstore, Shirley and another church member was coming in.

"Oh Hi! Deacon Zeek!"

Something inside of Zeek jumped as soon as he heard Shirley's voice.

His flesh tingled with pleasure at hearing her call his name and his heart panted as he gulped and responded, "Oh! Hi! Shirley."

"Deacon Zeek, this is Grace, she is a new member of the church. She switched her membership last Thursday night from one of those 'prosperity preaching' churches."

Grace brought her hand to her bosom, looking surprised, saying, "Shirley!"

"Well, it's a good church otherwise though Grace," Shirley said apologetically. "But anyway Grace, this is Deacon Zeek, the one who prayed for Bent Mike."

"Oh he is? Oh Hi Deacon. I heard so many good things about you. It's a pleasure meeting you," Grace replied excitedly.

"The pleasure is mines Sister Grace! Welcome to Zion. It's a joy having you here."

The Perfect Lesson

Grace smiled and elegantly handed Zeek her hand.

When Zeek held her uncommonly soft hand, and actually realized how tender her hand felt, before he knew it, his secret woke up. He prayed within himself that it would go down, but she squeezed his hand and he suffered much, trying hard to ignore what was happening to him for he enjoyed holding her hand. And Shirley made things worse with her wanting stare into Zeek's eyes.

"Thank you," Grace said smiling so innocently.

The tantalizing affect of her soft pleasant voice made Zeek's wrestle with his flesh very challenging, as by now, his secret became more awake, so much that he could not move without giving away the secret, of his secret's condition. So he grabbed his wrist with one hand while the other hand remained open in front, concealing his secret.

Unfortunately an annoying fly began buzzing around Zeek's head. His eyebrow and forehead began to desperately itch when the fly repeatedly landed about his forehead but he dared not to move his hands and become hugely embarrassed. So casually he shook his head so that maybe a wif of air may sooth the inching spot a bit. He fought not to look at Shirley and Grace soft shapely legs and partly exposed bosoms anymore, but Shirley's partially exposed bosom challenged him further till no end.

Young Darby

"Deacon if you need anything don't hesitate to call me," Shirley said smiling, as she began to walk away.

The Deacon began to wrestle with his flesh even more as they left and began speaking to himself in his mind saying, 'Why do they dress like that? Don't they know people look? Man! Oh man! Pastor need to preach on how people dress. Nevertheless, I rebuke you fleshly lust in the name of Jesus. I will not seek to commit adultery. I will not sin. I will not lust after Shirley or any other women anymore never again. I don't care how they dress. I have the mind of Christ. I am more then a conqueror, and I can do all things thru Christ who strengthens me. Greater is he that is in me then he who is in the world.'

Finally his secret was concealed.

"Wow! That was close," he said to himself and was on his way to his office.

Zeek worked at the church as the Treasurer and was very good at handling the church's finances for the last ten years. When Zeek reached the office, he made himself comfortable behind his desk, and called Ellen but only the answering machine came on. So he left a message: "Hi Sweety. I just called to let you know I'm at the office. I have already spoken

The Perfect Lesson

with the pastor and am now about to study the word for a minute. Call me when you can. Love you."

Deacon Zeek began his Bible reading, which went own for no less than two or three hours.

When he finished the phone rang. He watched it for a moment, when it got to the fourth rang he answered it.

"Deacon Zeek, may I help you?"

"Yes sir-ree! Deacon Zeek, I would like for you to preach the 4pm service tomorrow. I couldn't wait for you to call me and something else came up. I have to visit brother York; he's in the hospital. I don't know all of the details yet, but will fill you in as soon as I know his state. In the meanwhile, be in prayer mode for us."

"What's wrong with him?"

"Don't know yet. Said somethin' about doing exploratory surgery. Said it could be a number of things."

"Is he still smoking?"

"Yeah. Think so. You know how hard-headed he is."

"Did you get a chance to call Deacon Giz?"

"Yeah, but he wasn't in. I left a few massages on his machine, but you can past the info on to him too."

"OK Pastor. Peace and mercy be with you and Bro York. And give him my regards."

Young Darby

As the Deacon sat there at his desk he began visioning himself delivering the message on Sunday and all that he would say. The phone rang again. This time it was Deacon Giz.

"Brother Zeek. What's happening Big Brother?"

"Nothin' but the 'Word' man. Everything is fine by his grace."

"I see you gonna be preaching this Sunday at the 4 o'clock service."

"Yeah, that's right."

"That's cool, I might be preaching next Sunday at 4. Hey! Looka' here. You're not gonna preach we all got to be perfect right yet! Are you?"

"Why?"

"Cause I don't know how I'm gonna come on right behind an act like that."

"Well, depends on the Lord my brother. I might!"

"But Big Brother, don't you think it's a little too soon for that?"

"Not really. What's up like that?"

"Don't you think you should of, kind of, well, sought of, work the people up to that?"

"What ya' mean? I'm just gonna put it out there the way it is."

"Well I mean, even yourself as well? Cause I'm just gonna go a' head and tell you the truth man. Hey! You know me! Um from the old school."

"Yeah! I'm listening."

The Perfect Lesson

"Well brother Zeek, here's the deal: I don't believe no one can be perfect in this life like you're talkin' about. I agreed with what you were saying at first, when you told the pastor that no body could be perfect."

"Yeah I know I said that at first, but that was before I meditated on it and really took into account what the Rev was sayin', and after thinkin' about my own life, my own weaknesses and my own bad choices I've been making, know what I'm sayin'?"

"Zeek, I know you the head deacon and have to try and support the pastor regarding this perfection thing, but I want you to know that me and the brotherhood got your back. So if this perfection thing began to get to heavy for you, don't worry 'bout it buddy, me and the board will back you up all the way Big Brother. I still got some connections, you know!"

"The perfection piece aint the problem Giz."

"Well I'm just letting you know that most of us don't believe in that piece. Now maybe in the next life when we go to live with Jesus we would be perfect. But not right now, not here on this earth, on this planet, at this time! No-way Big Brother. But you can go ahead and preach it if you want, um just letting you know where I stand."

"I told you Giz, it depends on the Lord, and how he may lead me."

Young Darby

"Well you know the Lord aint gonna lead you to lie."

"To lie?"

"Yeah. You know what I'm talkin' bout."

"To lie about what?"

"Well you got to be perfect yourself to preach that people should be perfect. I know you aint sayin' that you are perfect already, are you?"

"No, I'm not saying that."

"That's' what I'm talkin' bout."

"Huh?"

"Look: I know the pastor scored some good points, and it all sounded good, but remember the point that you made?"

"What point was that?"

"You said that the tithes are gonna go down and you was gonna have to look for another job if he started preaching that perfect piece. I know you are the treasurer and all, but how many people you think gonna actually say Amen to someone telling them that they suppose to be perfect all the time, and if not, they're fakin' and going to hell? Huh?"

"Giz, I understand where you coming from. But God's word is what I'm preaching not mines. Nor will I preach to my own understanding.

God is the one who told us to be perfect, not me or the pastor. I know I use to be 'off the hook'. Those days are over. Now, I just want to do what's right before God. I want to do God's will."

The Perfect Lesson

"I hear ya' Big Brother. It was in the bible all the time but all of a sudden, Gateway told you that you suppose to be perfect, and instantly, 'Shazam' you're a perfect man, and gonna preach it too, huh? Jesus said it first and you aint do nothin' with it then."

Zeek did not respond.

"Or maybe you think the Rev is perfect or somethin' himself, huh?"

With contrary feelings beginning to mount about the discussion, Zeek shot, "If you really got a problem with it, you should pray about it and go take it up with God, I didn't right the book buddy. You don't want to be perfect you don't have too. That's your choice."

Now Giz began to fill a little upset. He paused, patiently inhaled, slowly exhaled then asked Zeek, "Have you seen Shirley lately Good Brother?"

"What? I mean, why?"

"I just ask a question that's all."

"What Shirley got to do with what we're talkin' about?"

"What so important about what we was talkin' about?"

"We were talkin' about God's Word. What's up?"

"I just wanted to see if you still had the 'hots' for her. That's all: especially now, that you're goin' all perfect on me and shit."

"Man you need prayer."

Young Darby

"Oh! Now I need prayer huh? But you do know she still lookin' don't ya'?."

"Giz you must have forgotten. I've repented about the past, been forgiven and God have blessed me with my own marvelous wife and that's that."

"Yeah! I know. You had your own marvelous wife when you was sayin' how fine Shirley fat ass was not to long ago too."

"Deacon Giz, that was the past. I done asked God's forgiveness about that too, repented and moved on."

"So you don't want to hit it no more, huh?"

"Man I can't believe we're discussing this," Zeek replied, as if offended, "I refuse to discuss the past any further. I repented about that and left it in the Lord's hands and that's it. Why you doing this man?"

"So you believe God done forgave you for everything you ever done wrong and regardless of how many times you done jack-off bout Shirley?"

"What? You of all people should know the goodness of the Lord and what his forgiveness is all about. You tryin' send me on a guilt trip right? And you never jacked-off?"

"Naw! I'm just stating the ungodly facts to somebody that's about to preach that I got to be perfect or I'm gonna die and go to hell. You damn right um sending you on a guilt trip. Tell you the truth, Sound like you already tripin'."

The Perfect Lesson

"Well I know one thing, I aint tripping no mo'. Talk to you later when you not so upset and on a fault finding mission."

"Zeek, now you know me and you go way back to the hood buddy. Don't start the holier-than-thou stuff with me."

"The truth is the light Giz. It aint like you don't have any house-cleaning to do yourself."

"One thing about me, I can proudly and truthfully say, Big Brother, I'm not perfect, aint tryin' to be and don't wanna be. And I aint gonna be perpetrating, teaching folk to be perfect when I know damn well I'm not and they don't have to be."

"Um um um. I can't believe it."

"Understand what I'm saying?"

"Only thing I understand is that you don't wanna do God's perfect will. You just want to keep on sinning."

"You got some nerve! Well anyway, since you have become Mr. Goody Two Shoes over night, Shirley said she saw you today. I bet you was horny as hell when you saw her wasn't you?"

"What?" Zeek said with a surprised look on his face.

"She asked me to ask you to come and pray for her tonight if you have time. I told her I would ring you."

"Yeah thanks. I'll be praying for you too. Later!"

Young Darby

"You don't need to pray for me. I'm OK. I'm particular anyway."

"Oh! Yeah?"

"Don't worry 'bout it. Talk to you later Good Brother! Bye."

They both hung up, sore at each other. Zeek struck a heavy blow to his desk with his fist, quietly yelling, "Damn Giz! I can't believe that asshole talked to me like that."

On the other end, Giz was reared back in his 'lazy boy' thinking of how he could bring Zeek down a peg or two. In an instant seemingly, a light came on in Giz's head. He whipped out the church's missionary roster and found just who he was thinking of and proceeded to dial her up. He waited with crossed fingers for her to answer the phone. It ranged the six time, and...."Yes!" he went.

"Hello! Shirley! May I help you?"

"Hi Honeybunch! This is, Giz."

"Oh! Hi Deacon."

"I told you Sis Shirley, you could just call me Giz. We just chatting over the phone, you know? You see, I like to keep it real: you know what I mean?"

"Ok! I'm sorry. But did you get a chance to talk to Deacon Zeek?"

"I sure did. He said he would be glad to come over. He also wondered why you didn't ask him yourself."

The Perfect Lesson

"Oh really?"

"Well you know Zeek, uhm Deacon Zeek! He love himself some Shirley"

"What! He said that too?"

"Well, it's like this baby, Deacon don't talk to too many people. He sought to like to keep his thoughts to himself but sometimes he tells me stuff."

"I'm sure he didn't mean nothin' by it."

"I don't know about that."

"Deacon Zeek is a happily married man with a beautiful sweet wife. I know he aint mean nothin'."

"I hope you're right. But he did say whenever he see you, he becomes warm all over and have to sat down."

"Warm? Have to sit down? Why? For what?"

"Uhm. Oh my goodness! I didn't mean to tell you that, cause I know you goin' to go tell him. And he gonna be saying Deacon Giz don't know how to keep nothin', dag!" Giz said, trying not to let Shirley hear him chuckling.

"Oh no! I won't do that Deacon Giz. My lips are sealed."

"Promise?"

"I promise. Plus that would embarrass him and may cause strife between the two of you. I wouldn't dare do that. Everybody know you two are best of friends and y'all just work so well together."

"Yep! Got to admit it, he's alright with me."

Young Darby

"Did he say anything else?"

"Well only that when you get just a little bit close to him or touch him even with your coat, he said he goes wild with the sin of covetousness."

"What you say Deacon?"

"Now, Shirley hon, I aint saying no more. I already said too much. Now this is between you and me Shirley."

"Oh my goodness gracious Deacon. What I'm going to do with that man? Bless his heart."

"I tell you, he's somthin' else. I know I won't have to worry about you telling anyone about this since you promised. I know by faith you would keep your promise and not gossip, so we cool: right?"

"Yeah! We cool!" Shirley said, shaking her head, "But Deacon Giz, I mean Giz, I don't know what to do when he come over here."

"Just be your same charming self."

"And you still didn't tell me why I make him want to sit down!"

The Deacon covered the phone with his hand so she could not hear how badly he could not keep from sniggering. And his belly jumped and shirked at each muffled explosion of hidden laughs and conniving sinister snicker.

"Deacon? Giz? You still there?"

"Oh yes baby, I'm here," he said, while struggling to control his snickering. "Shirley 'honey'," he

The Perfect Lesson

said, as if he was coughing, and trying to clear his throat, "Uhm, um! Oh boy! I was just.....I was just trying to get something. Well, I'm going to let you go now baby, I know you got something else to do besides listen to me. And I got a few things to catch up on myself."

"Ok Deacon, but any time, you know me and you talk."

"Ok! So call me tomorrow my dear."

"Ok Deacon, and thanks for the information."

"Anytime love."

After Giz hung-up the phone, he sat there with a proud smile stretching from ear to ear. As he sat there sniggering still, he felt a certain level of satisfaction, as well as payback and contentment. He stood-up and pulled-up his pants on his fairly rounded hanging belly and was feeling pretty good with himself.

Giz was on the heavy side of the scale, at about 5ft 9 and weighed about 190 pounds, give or take a few, with most of it showing up in his mid section. But since he wore baggy trousers with dark tops a lot, it was sometimes hard to guess his weight. His face was dark and skinny with rather big lips and egg sized eyes. Because of the broad size of his nose, when he talked or ate, his nostril would flare open, so if you were looking directly at him, you would be also looking into his nose.

Young Darby

It was approaching dust, and Deacon Zeek was about to leave his office after a long day of study and accounting.

He put his hand on the doorknob and when he turned it, he remembered that he supposed to pray for Shirley. He put his things down and began praying right there where he stood.

"Oh Lord, please be with me Dear God! Anoint me with a double portion of your holy spirit, and lead me that I might not sin. Lord, I know you hate sin. But sometimes my flesh desire that which is sin. It's not me, but my flesh Lord that craves and wants it all the time. My flesh craves even against the knowledge of my mind. And my flesh has no control of itself, understanding or knowledge, but just want, and is filled with irrational desire and it wages war even against the truth that I know, against even the righteousness in me, against godliness, even against my own self-control. I spend a large part of my time just fighting this personal war and I struggle to keep control so that my flesh do not rule me for a day or for an hour. Father God, I seem to be losing this fight. Please help me Lord. It seems like after that meeting in the field with pastor, lust has been taking a hold of me. Oh Lord and my God, show me how to walk as you? Or even if I could at least walk as my pastor. Help me Lord. Help me

The Perfect Lesson

to overcome this lust that's always tempting me. Speak to my situation before I sin a great sin. Take it away from me Lord or give me the wisdom to deal with it as I should. Lord I sought you on other occasions so that you would strengthen me in this area. Lord, but it's still hunting me. I've been to the altar, I prayed, I fasted Lord. What is it that I'm doing wrong? Oh Lord, I know I suppose to preach this coming Sunday, and I'm contemplating sinfully already. Lord, please help me.

In Jesus name I pray, Amen. Oh Lord, bless Shirley and give her the desires of her heart and make our relationship a right one. In Jesus name, Amen."

He hesitated for a moment then went back to his desk. He looked up Shirley's phone number: found it and dialed her up, but yet, hoping that she was not in so he could leave a massage on the answering machine.

The phone rang the sixth time, the seventh time, the eighth and the answering machine picked up. He breathed out a sigh of relief and eagerly left the massage saying:

"Hi Sister Shirley! This is Deacon Zeek. Deacon Giz said you asked for a visit. I was calling to see if you where in since we did not confirm a definite

Young Darby

time, and it's getting late. Nevertheless, I will pray for you anyway and as you know, distance can't affect the power of a fervent prayer, so call me when you can. God bless you. Bye"

Shirley sat there in her room looking at her caller ID and listening to the massage, and an uneasy feeling pervaded her. Butterflies filled her stomach. She searched her feelings for the Deacon. And discovered deep admiration. She fancied a 'fling' with him, but it so soon fizzled. But she wanted to see him regardless of her unresolved bearings, but did not know how to go about it. For Shirley's late husband had died five years ago due to an alcoholic related disease. Since then, she lived alone and often prayed day and night that the Lord would send her a God fearing man.

After the Deacon finished praying, he went home. After dinner he and Ellen began their daily routine of rehashing their day together.

Meanwhile Deacon Giz was at home brainstorming away to win Zeek back or to teach him a lesson which lead him to decide to call the pastor.

The Perfect Lesson

The phone rang a few times before the Pastor Gateway answered.

"Greetings, Gateway may I help you?"

"Yes sir! How ya' doing, Pastor?"

"Great! Are you ready for tomorrow Deacon?"

"Yes sir! That's what I called you about."

"What's up?"

"I see you have Deacon Zeek in the lined up for the 4 O'clock service tomorrow"

"Yes I do."

"Do you really think he's up to it?"

"What make you ask that?"

"He just seemed so busy lately."

"Oh, don't worry. He'll be fine. That Deacon got nothin' but the power of God working in him. I saw it in his eyes in the field just before he left."

"Uhm."

"By the way, have you seen him or spoken to him this evening?"

"Nope, but I believe I know where he is."

"Yeah! He's probably at home in the bed, If not in the word. He has to give a sure fire word tomorrow, you know?"

"That's right pastor, but I don't think he's home."

"Well, where else could he be this time of night?"

"I believe he's still over Sister Shirley's."

Young Darby

"What!" Gateway said tenoring his voice, "What he's doing over there this time of night?"

"Don't get me lying, Pastor. That Deacon is somethin' else I tell you!"

"Hummm, that fellow should be home by now!"

"Ok Pastor I don't want to keep you up: just wanted to check on you that's all."

"Well Thanks Giz. I really appreciate that. See you tomorrow Deacon Giz, the Lord's will, and thanks again for calling me. May God's peace be with you."

"Ok Pastor. God Bless you too!"

Deacon Giz snuggled in his chair and began to feel even a greater since of satisfaction and success as he hung-up the phone, now that he had put that bug in the pastor's ear. Then he knelled and began his night time prayer:

"Oh God, I thank you for making me like you did, without guile or lies. Sometimes, I may exaggerate a little, but you know Lord, sometime you have to help people to get the point. For your word say's be as wise as a snake, but as harmless as a dove. And I'm trying Lord. And if you see anything not right in me Lord, take it far from me. I'm just trying to show brother Zeek he aint perfect, never was perfect, and aint never gonna be perfect, and help restore him back on track so that he wont be lost. Open up his eyes Lord and let him see Lord that he can't be perfect. Lord, I don't know what's

The Perfect Lesson

wrong with him! Lord show him that it aint no body perfect down here and aint nobody trying to be perfect but him.

So Lord, please help him to understand today. I pray Lord in the name of Jesus. Ho ma shawnda, He Ma shawnda....Oh my my my shawnda shawnda....... And Dear Lord, bring Deacon Zeek to the truth of your word. Show him that it aint no way that he or no one else is gonna never ever be perfect aside from the way I told him, and not like he think you said. Hallelujah. Thank you Lord.... Thank ya' Jesus Amen"

It was an early Sunday morning. The birds were chirping non-stop, colorful butterflies flew rampant. The outdoor freshly scented pine breezes of soft winds parted the curtains of the pastor's windows, which delightfully woke him. He immediately got out of the bed, kneeled at the foot of his bed, as was his habit, thanked the Lord for keeping him and allowing him to be in the land of the living for another day. Gateway then stood up, stretched and sighed, "Oh boy," and went over and stood in front of the bedroom window peering out at the trees, the birds, and butterflies, and said, "All of the visible handy-works of the All Mighty God on display thru my window.

Young Darby

What did I do to deserve this? Why me, Lord? Lord, I thank you. Oh well let' me get myself together and get busy. I can since a powerful word from the Lord today. My stars look at the time!"

And he made haste getting ready, and was on his way while singing, 'Thank You Lord! Thank You Lord. I Just Want To Thank You Lord!

The first person he met in the parking lot after he drove up and parked, was Deacon Zeek.

"Brother Zeek! Halleluiah!"

They got out of their car and greeted each other with a hearty hug, shared some encouraging words, entered into the church, and went their own respective ways to their own offices in preparation for services. Today time was just moving too fast for Pastor Gateway. He sat there in his office as if he could still smell the pine scent from his bedroom window or would atleast like to, as he slowly inhaled with a pleasant expression of peace holding his face. "Boy, where did the time go?" he said, as he got up and started walking towards the sanctuary. He notice today that everyone he greeted along the way to the sanctuary, though they spoke and exchanged pleasant greetings, they all seemed to have had a covert agenda or some concealed concerns and some of the faces seem to reflect a hint

The Perfect Lesson

of many worries. These conditions seemed to have vividly manifest theirselves in colors of spiritual tones to the pastor today, as he met and greeted the members and visitors along the way, so much so that by the time he reached the pulpit he had to kneel down to meditate and regenerate himself in prayer a few minutes or more at the altar before directing the services. Afterwards, he instructed the choir director, who directed the musicians and choir to began. The selections included such hymns as: I Surrender All, I'm A Soldier In The Army Of The Lord, Leaning On The Everlasting Arm and This Little Light Of Mine which was the last of the opening song at this 11oclock service.

The church was packed past seating capacity, with people standing in the back along the walls and on both-sides of the walls. People were also seated in the lobby, some standing and looking thru the lobby's doors on this very warm Easter Sunday. The Pastor looked around at his Deacons after the song, 'This Little Light Of Mine', ended. The pastor stood-up shaking his head, slowly repeating the title of the song: 'This Little Light Of Mine'.

Looking up as if looking through the church's ceiling, and he said, "I'm going to let it shine. How many of you out there are goin' to really let your light shine everyday of life?" An astounding symphony of 'Amen' and shouts flooded the sanctuary. "Hold it now. Wait a minute, don' don'

Young Darby

don't say that if you don't mean it. You see," he said as he positioned himself in center stage in a power stance and continued, "The Lord hates untruths. A lot of you was singing that song because you liked the way it sounded. You didn't sing it for what it meant. You know you're not really gonna let your light shine everywhere you go. Some of you don't let your light shine anywhere. In fact, many people that a lot of you know, don't even know you have the light. But you are singing it anyway. Some of you didn't let your light shine on your way here today, did ya? 'You, song a lie!' Most of you know good and well, you're not gonna shine your light even when you leave this place today.

The congregation was bubbling with words of encouragement saying, "Preach on! Tell the truth!" and "Tell the story." The Pastor continued.

"You song a lie!' Most of us are not going to tell anybody about Jesus Christ except for the people we already know, aint it right Deacons? So you, song a lie!" the pastor said looking into Deacon's Giz eyes. Deacon Giz smiled and shouted along with the other deacons, "Amen Rev! Preach the gospel."

The Pastor went on, "You're not gonna pray for the leaders of this world nor have you been praying for them in the past, have you? But yet, you're singing the song. Now if I'm right something wrong. Tell the truth, you don't give-a-damn, do you?"

The Perfect Lesson

'Ous' and 'awes' were heard throughout the sanctuary, but the pastor continued:

"You know there are people living in sin all around you, but you have not been praying for their souls, have ya'? A lot of you who are singing these songs are still committing fornication and some, adultery, aint you? Are you hearing me? Can I park right here on: 'Don't 'Wantabe Street', for a minute?" The Pastor paused, sat down for a moment, and looked into the eyes of many of the members, choir members, missionaries, deacons and those that set in the pulpit that where standing, and those seated behind him.

When all became quiet again, he wiped the sweat from his forehead, stood-up and carefully proceeded, "There is a difference between the two. Fornication is when you and your partner are not married or never been married and you have sex with them: and saying you love each other aint got nothing to do with it. This is a sin in the sight of God. I don't care how much you say you love each other. And God said no fornicator would inherit the Kingdom of Heaven. Adultery, is when both or one of the partners are married to someone or were at one time married to someone else who is not deceased or was not separated from their spouse according to the scripture and is having sex with someone other than their spouse. This is sin in the eyes of God and is worthy of damnation and hell

Young Darby

fire and causes a great horrific stink in the nostrils of a holy God. Am I making it plain?"

Most of the older members shouted, "Amen! Preach on!"

The pastor continued, "Ladies and gentlemen, God despise sin. But loves righteousness. If you did not know what fornication and adultery was or is, today you know!"

The church became so quiet that you could hear a pin drop. The Pastor continued, "Boy! This place sure got quiet all of a sudden. What did I say? Well anyway turn your Bibles to......No.no…no…. Let's do this. Turn your hearts to God and come quickly to the altar." A crowd came to the altar but many remained seated with looks of contentment. Some wore mean looks. Some wore frowns. Some looked scared and some inconspicuously slipped out of the church doors during the movement of those going to the altar. When all became settled, the Pastor prayed for the protection, security, health, peace wisdom and unmovable steadfastness of faith in Christ for his flock. When done, all that went to the altar returned to their seats as if spiritually regenerated. After an instrumental selection (Hold Out) the pastor extended an invitation for all to come forward and receive Jesus Christ as Lord and Savior of their life, but no one answered the invitation and the service was concluded.

Chapter 8
How Can I Preach With Lust

Deacon Zeek could not wait to reach his office, but once he did, he went and sat at his desk, and began exhaling with a sigh of welcomed relief.

He began asking God to allow someone else to preach in his place, and started feeling doubt, low esteemed and quilt ridden within himself, for he feared that Giz was right, that lust had gotten the best of him, and maybe he was not ready to preach the truth yet, especially since he was not perfect himself. He seemed to acknowledge that there was a more excellent word from the Lord but felt prohibited from preaching it. He looked at the clock, checked it by his watch. It was now 2pm, only 2 hours before his turn. Time was going to fast he thought. He began to force himself to breath-in deeply to force out the nervousness engulfing him. In his office with the doors closed, he even tried some of the old Ti Chi exercises that he use to do, but that didn't help much either. So he felt that he should leave for a few minutes, and go somewhere so maybe he could shout if he felt the need for such an outlet. He managed to slip out of the building without being called or given another matter to

Young Darby

work on or think about. The only one that noticed he slipped out was Delores, but she said nothing.

Zeek drove to the place where the Pastor called that out-door meeting about a mile and a half from the church a few days ago to meet with the Deacons.

He parked along the roadside, mostly on the grassy area, breathed with relief, got out the car and began pacing across the field. He began recalling their talks about being perfect as the Father is perfect. He noticed, as he thought about perfection this time, it did not have the same impact as it did at first when the pastor was there. He felt alone, so began to metacognized. And as he thought on what he was actually feeling and thinking he concluded that his motivation was low because he had not resolve what he would do if he and Shirley were to be together alone. So he began to talk to God about the matter:

"Father if I had a chance, I think I would enjoy kissing and holding that fine lady Lord. So how can I preach Lord? And what about that woman? Please speak to me Lord. Please speak to my situation. I'm already married and love my wife. I know you hear and see what I'm going through as well as what I'm doing".

The Perfect Lesson

The deacon kneeled down, laid out his case before the Lord and continued to plead and pray to the Lord for more strength.

Back at the church, Pastor Gateway was looking for the deacon to pray with him.

"Has anybody seen Deacon Zeek?" he inquired of his staff.

No one seemed to have known where he was. And when Deacon Giz realized that Zeek was not in his office, he began to look for him too. He even called Shirley, but she informed him that she have not heard from, or seem him since the earlier service.

It was now approaching 4pm and Delores was worried and prayed what she should do. So for now, she tried to stay out of the pastor way, so he would not ask her if she had seen Deacon Zeek because she knew she could not lie. Now the pastor concern was growing and becoming obvious as he began to ask the deacon's whereabouts as if placing blame on those he asked. Before long, it was just minutes before 4oclock. The doors of the church were open, and in a short while the church again was filled to capacity.

Then the official body and all attending auxiliaries where in place and the choir began to

Young Darby

sing, 'Zion, Zion, Beautiful, Beautiful Zion'. The entire sanctuary was filled with adoration, tears, looks of happiness, and humility, and the voices of the masses resounded beautifully through the roof as they sang.

Before long, the side-door opened; the pastor was startled and even more so when Deacon's Zeek head slowly emerged. Deacon Zeek confidently slipped in thru the side entry and onto the pulpit. Deacon Giz looked disappointed when he saw Zeek. Shirley was happy when she saw him, and Ellen, who sat next to Shirley today on the third row from the front was glowing with pride. The Pastor was so glad to see Zeek that when Zeek reached the pulpit, the pastor rubbed and patted him on his back, and hugged him as though it had been years since he last seen him. Deacon Zeek sat and kneeled his head while inwardly praying. Deacon Giz could not hide his look of contempt for Zeek, so he kept looking around throughout the congregation as if looking for someone in order to hide his frowns and expression of contempt, but smiled ever so gently at Zeek's wife when his roaming eyes bumped into hers.

After the Welcome Announcements, and a few hymns, Deacon Zeek stood-up to preach.

He began by saying, "Glory be to God, the Father and to his Son Jesus Christ who has given

The Perfect Lesson

us this day, and has given me this opportunity to come before you."

He paused and looked into his wife's eyes, but his eyes also fell on Shirley, for she was setting right beside Ellen today. For a very brief moment in his mind, he could see himself alone with Shirley, desiring her and seeing himself being strong resisting her until she accidentally touched his secret, and then he saw himself rebuking himself. He placed a handkerchief over his mouth and said to the congregation, "Ya'll pray for me, I'm coming."

He paused again and in his mind, this time, he saw Shirley with a revealing see-through blue blouse and a silky white mini slip on, blushing and saying to him, 'Do you really want me?'

And he heard himself answering, 'Yes!'

Now the Deacon felt the weight of the world on his shoulders and said again to the congregation aloud, "Pray for me. The Lord is good."

This time he spoke with tears, confusion and weakness. When he began to speak at the next moment, he noticed Deacon Giz was setting propped stylishly back in his seat looking right into his mouth with an astute look, as if he dared him to preach perfection. Then he suddenly saw Giz saying to him in a vision, 'You aint shit, and you never was shit, and you will never be nothing but a sinner so don't even try it.

Young Darby

I'll tell your wife on your holy ass, and spread all of your shit in the street if you preach that perfection stuff. What you doing up there in the pulpit in the first place. Talkin' bout you like women with fat asses! Who do you think you foolin' boy? I will tell on your sanctified ass anyhow. You call yourself a Deacon do you?'

Deacon Zeek reluctantly lifted his head and looked out into the congregation, as if looking for help. And the expression, 'Help me,' was written all over his face and Ellen recognized it, and sat with baited breath, for she did not understand why he looked this way at this moment. Zeek finally continued, "Church, you all look so good and so well dressed today. But most importantly is, that you all have repented of your sins. Of course you are all probably going to heaven. I know there is many things we like to have and need down here, and we can get them. In fact, God want us to have all of the things we desire as long as those things wont hurt us. Don't you know you can have it if you ask and believe?

The Title of this message is, 'The Lord is Good'. You see, God love all of us and want to give us everything we desire and to keep us from all trouble. And don't you know, when you learn how to pray, you can get anything you want from God? You see, my God said that he would supply all of your needs and give you the desire of your

The Perfect Lesson

heart. You see my brothers and sisters, our heavenly father is rich and own everything. He will heal your body, and make away out of no way."

The 'Amens' and the 'Hallelujahs' came pouring in from all throughout the congregation.

Many stood-up from their chair and Giz was smiling from ear to ear, shouting, "Praise God! Preach it preacher," and clapping his hands. Then he sat down and stood back-up, shouting, "Preach the Gospel."

Pastor Gateway dropped his head. Delores watched the pastor as he secretly wiped the tears from his eyes, tightening his lips and nodding his head slowly from left to right with misty eyes searching the congregation, but the congregation seeing his tears, took it to mean that the pastor was in so much agreement with what was being preached, that he was dripping tears of joy.

Deacon Zeek noticed how Shirley eyes glowed, and from where he stood he could see her shinny, shapely legs, silky smooth knees and part of her thigh. He could not fight the thoughts that flooded his mind of foundling, holding and kissing her upon her cinnamon laid shoulders, on down to her refined golden ankles. His lustful appetite was only weakened by him feeling uneasy seeing his wife sitting beside Shirley, and he wondered how much they talked and what they talked about.

Young Darby

Zeek continued, "My brothers and sisters, in the Lord, we got to be strong and go on with the Lord's work. He put us all here for a special reason, so no matter what comes up we must stay the course. The road may not be easy but we got to fight with all of our might. Sometimes you gonna feel like quitin' but you got to keep on being strong anyway. Jesus had to fight temptation so we are gonna have to fight temptation too. Yes! And I believe we will stay the course because we have some God fearing people in this house that is destined for heavenly glory. There are going to be many trials and tribulations but we must be strong. And matter of fact, I believe today is your day to receive a special blessing and boost from the Lord. If you believe this stand-up on your feet and shout, 'Amen'."

All over the sanctuary people was standing and praising God, but when he turned around to look at the ministers standing behind him in the pulpit, he noticed that Pastor Gateway was not there.

Deacon Zeek continued, "That's all I have to say. But before I go, I just want you to know, that you got to keep the faith, and just do the best you can and everything will be alright."

"Amen," was echoed through-out the sanctuary. Deacon Giz stood-up clapping, confirming Deacon's Zeek message, and saying to those around him, "That man preach this morning didn't he?"

The Perfect Lesson

The other deacons also stood and clapped, saying, "Amen! Hallelujah!"

The pastor was in his office in sorrow and bewildered. On his feet he stood, alone in his office, and began to question God, as if he was talking to the person of God, face to face, saying, "Lord, what was that all about? What happened Father? Zeek is a child after your own heart. He showed me and told me so in so-many words. Why did he not preach your words Lord? The 'word' that you have confirmed and given unto us on this day. How come he didn't preach it? Help me Holy Father to understand? Is the Devil so strong as to cause this? Lord, something is wrong and I need to know what it is. That was not the Zeek I know. Father, I'm leaving this matter in your hands and I would really appreciate an answer today, alright Father?"

In the sanctuary, Deacon Giz was again smiling from ear to ear, as if he had just hit the 'jack pot'. He hurried to greet the sweating anxious Zeek. And around about this time, Zeek was feeling so relieved that his sermon was done that he could hardly wait to go home. He didn't even want to stop by his office for fear that he might see Gateway. He motioned to Ellen to come and when she joined him he told her to go and start the car because he was a bit tired.

Ellen replied, "Aren't you goin' to say 'bye' to pastor?"

Young Darby

"He's probably tied-up right now baby. He always gets tied-up after service, so go-ahead baby start the car up so we won't get blocked in. Plus I don't think I parked right today."

"Looks like you parked alright to me."

Zeek began to speed-up shacking hands as he saw Giz approaching, for neither did he care to speak or greet Giz at this time. Deacon Zeek soon noticed out the corner of his eye that the pastor was coming in his direction.

Without looking directly in the pastor's line of direction, Zeek grabbed Ellen by the waist and casually and gently guided her to the door and out to the car, hoping only that the pastor would not notice him as he briefly shook a few more hands and slipped into the cluster of people in the church lobby doorway, then briskly move on his way to his car among the crowd.

"Dear honey, I still think you should atleast let him know you're leaving, he may want to see you about somethin'," Ellen said as she put on her seatbelt.

"You may be right baby, I'll call him once I think he settled down. By-the-way, how long have you've been knowing Shirley?"

"Oh, not long. She doesn't talk much unless she really have something to say. She seems to keep to herself most of the time. Why you ask that?"

The Perfect Lesson

"Oh, nothing. I think that was the first time I saw you two setting together."

Back at the church, Gateway was combing the area for Zeek and asking practically everyone in sight have they seen him. This time Delores informed him that Zeek left minutes ago. The Pastor just stood there as if trying to figure out why Zeek message was so mundane and contrary to all that they spoke about, and then left without a word of good-bye.

"Did he say anything, or that he was coming back?"

"No Sir," said Delores staring into the Pastor's eyes as if looking for the answer in the pastor's eyes herself.

Zeek finally reached home and was digging in to a loaded salad when his phone ranged.

"Ella, get that please. If that's the pastor tell him I'll call him right back!"

'Zeek…. Zeek…Zeek!"

"Yes Dear!"

"It's the pastor!"

Young Darby

"Sweetheart, I told you to…..Ahhhh shi..boy… shucks. Ok," Zeek said rubbing his forehead, paused for a moment, took a few deep breaths, then with a reluctant struggle, and after exhaling his tension, grabbed the phone.

"Hello Pastor how are you feeling?"

"What happen to you today, Zeek?"

"Sir?"

"What happen to that sure word we were in agreement about?"

"What ya' talkin' bout pastor? I preached today."

"What you preached about?"

"You didn't hear the whole message. You left before you heard everything."

"Yeah I left."

"Why did you leave?"

"What part did I miss?"

"Um."

"Did I miss the part where you spoke of doing the total will of God and how we show we love God by keeping his word and what he commands?"

"Well..."

"Did I miss that part?"

There was a brief silence on the phone.

"Zeek, are you still there?.....Deacon Zeek?"

Zeek inhaled deeply, slowly exhaling his tension, answered, "Yeah, I'm here Pastor, but Pastor, sometimes the Lord can lead you differently from what you may be planning on doing."

"Zeek, I need to see you."
"Oh' uh…ok."
"When can you come by?"
"How about next week Pastor?"
"Or should I come over there?
"Its up to you Pastor."
"We need to talk about somethin' Brother."
"Let me look at my schedule and take care of something first Pastor, then I'll call you back."
"Ok Deacon, don't keep me waiting too long."
"Ok, I wont," Zeek muttered.
"Alright, Zeek."
"Ok Pastor."

Got to meet with the Pastor about the sermon

Zeek sat back in his chair thinking about how he was going to respond to the Pastor and began to examine his conscience.

He began to pray, "Lord, what's wrong with me? Why can't I turn completely away from my lustful desires? What happened to my strength and those mighty scriptures that suppose to have been embedded into my mind and at work in me? Why are these feelings of lust so strong within me? Help me to be stronger then they are. Your word says that I'm more than a conqueror and that I can do all things through Christ. How come I'm not acting like it? Why lust keep overcoming me? Even

Young Darby

though lust keeps challenging me, I still believe that I am more then a conqueror, because greater is he that is in me, than he that is in the world. Lord I'm gonna fight this thing. Lust will not rule me. In Jesus name, I Pray. Amen."

Zeek picked up the phone and called the pastor and they settled for a meeting on Tuesday at 2pm on the field. After Zeek pondered over his condition for a while, he felt relieved and informed Ellen of his meeting with the pastor and told her to not let him forget it.

Ellen said, "Ok! Good Dear!" Herself too, feeling relieved knowing that Zeek was going to meet with the pastor. For she was bothered in thinking that Zeek may have been avoiding the pastor for some reason. Ellen suddenly remembered that she and missionary Gladys suppose to visit a few hospitalized members this evening and give Deacon Giz a report on Monday, so she quickly located and placed a chicken potpie in the oven for Zeek's dinner.

"Oh dear, I just remembered, I suppose to be visiting the sick today and I'm late. A chicken pie is in the oven and the timer is on. Please listen for the, 'ding' and help yourself," she said mindfully, with her coat half on and one foot halfway in the other shoe, as she limped towards the door working one shoe on her foot at the sametime. Zeek dashed to the door while she struggled to put the shoe on

The Perfect Lesson

and quickly kissed her off, and Ellen was on her way. By the time Zeek had gotten him a drink, and parked in front of the tube, Ellen was pulling off. When he started sipping his drink and surfing the tube good, the phone rang.

"Hello!"

"Hello Big Brother! Guess whose over here 'Good-buddy'?

"Shirley!"

"Awh man, you're hot! But not hot enough."

"Who?"

"Just try. I bet you a million dollars you can't guess!"

"Bent Mike!"

"Naw man. Give you a clue: you haven't seen her since last communion!"

"You got me Giz. I give up. Who is it?"

"Tell you what, I'm getting ready to drop her off somewhere, but we'll swing by your place first for a hot second and you can just say, 'Hey'."

"That's ok Giz, don't let me hold you up, I can see who it is later."

"No bother, Big Brother she's already out there in the car waiting for me. We'll be over in a few minutes, and ma—-n, please forgive me about my attitude yesterday, you know I'm only human and besides man, me and you go way back. You know we still down."

Young Darby

"Really Giz It's not a good time to come by right now, I was just ……"

"Awe man we wont even get out of the car, we'll just blow the horn. Then you can just peep out at the car and say, 'Hello' or somethin'. Man, I got a surprise for you. Just one minute of your time. I promise!"

"Alright!"

"My man!"

The Set-Up

Giz was bubbling with delight in anticipation of seeing the old Zeek and couldn't get in the car fast enough to zoom over to Zeek's place, especially since it was now evident that Zeek was not going to be preaching that perfection piece: and everything will remain the same, just as Giz always wanted.

The oven's timer rang and Zeek had done took the potpie out and got back comfortable in front of the tube and had begun digging in with one hand and surfing with the other, but before he could get midway into the pie, someone was knocking on the door.

Zeek wondered who it was, because he hasn't been to long talking to Giz. And Giz normally takes

The Perfect Lesson

his times when he tells someone he's coming over: plus Giz suppose to honk his horn, so it couldn't be him.

Zeek peeped through the peephole and sure enough he was surprise when he saw Giz grinning and smiling from ear to ear. Curiosity took hold of Zeek and he flung open the door. When Zeek saw who was with Giz, he stood speechless with his mouth wide-open as he looked on. Giz asked, "Can we come in for one moment, we wont be a minute. I just knew you might want to say 'Hi' to Sister Judy before I take her back," Giz said, while secretly winking at Zeek while Judy wasn't looking.

Zeek heart began racing by the seconds, and his hormonal level was rising quicker then ever as he spoke, "Well Oh hi Sister Judy! It is a joy seeing you."

Judy shyly snuck a peep down at Zeek's crouch, and Zeek noticed. She walked with her body swaying back and fourth as she drew towards him saying, "Deacon Giz said you been asking about me and if I have any problems I should see you first and that the pastor also recommend you."

Deacon Zeek experienced another speechless moment as he immediately looked at Giz as if waiting for an explanation.

"Well, well Deacon Zeek I was just telling her the best I could, you know! After all, everybody knows about Steve and Bent Mike. Could I see your phone one minute?"

"Yeah, sure," Zeek said, staring at Giz still as Giz went pass him and into the dinning room to use the phone. When Zeek turned back around he noticed Judy was standing there blushing, and Zeek became as putty. Judy butt was perfectly round, shapely and wobbled with any and every movement that she made, just as Zeek always fantasized the ideal shape and composition for a woman anatomy. Her breast was huge and pointing at the tips with the top part of her breast exposed so that if she were to bend over, you could see her bosom in full hanging view. Her skirt was so short, Zeek was afraid to ask her to sit down for fear of seeing an impression of her secret. Her legs seemed to have been smoother than silk. Judy was the epitome of all that Zeek could ever hope for in any of his fiendish fantasies. He tried hard to control his breathing in-order not to show his lust when he spoke, which he felt surfacing at an uncontrollable and over bearing rate. When he smiled at her, she gracefully swayed by him and turned about admiring his colorful African art work and wall paintings. He watched her every move and gesture as if she was a movie and his breathing became shallower. He prayed within himself that the Lord would give him strength right now at this moment of weakness to not embarrass himself. And as soon as he felt some symbolists of strength

The Perfect Lesson

coming, Judy looked at him with a soft innocent smile, sat down and slowly yet properly crossed her legs and broke the silence:

"Deacon Zeek, I know I don't have an appointment and you are very busy, but can I make an appointment to see you later this week in private?"

Zeek sat there looking sincere, but yet could not help but see her pinkies and her upper thighs due to the way her legs were crossed. With his lust stricken throat, Zeek said, "Yes my dear!

Just call me a few days ahead of time and I will be more than glad to help you out as best I can. That's what I'm here for my dear."

Judy leaned forward, rubbed and petted him gently on the inner thigh of his leg with a friendly smile and thanked him but she left her hand resting on his leg near his crouch as if she needed to do so in-order to support herself as she bent down to rub her ankle bracelet and her bosoms became exposed to Zeek's now hungry awaiting desire seeking eyes. Awe, Zeek's jaws dropped, as he embraced these fleeting tantalizing moments with intense inflamed desire, as his eyes dotted and searched to capture the complete circumference of Judy's luscious robustious hanging bubs and savoring every moment in wantingness.

Zeek began questioning himself about why she was doing this to him. For he thought to himself that she must have known what she was doing to some degree. But he didn't care, he only wanted to see more and for Giz to stay in the other room. And his secret betrayed him, so he calmly tried to hide it without looking. For he thought if she caught him looking, she would look at it too and find out. Therefore he was unsuccessful in concealing his bulging secret completely. Zeek finally felt like this situation was too much for him to tolerate. He asked himself again, 'Why is this happening to me? She must know what she's doing to me. She must want it too. I know she want it. Oh my Lord. Lord please don't let her see what's happening to me.'

To distract her, Zeek pointed with his head at the coffee table behind Judy, and said, "Judy! Judy! Oh Judy! You sure are so welcome.

Just write my number on somethin' over their cause I just might be able to set up something earlier with you!"

"Oh boy that would be good," Judy said as she looked over at the coffee table.

"Anytime my dear. And I'm so glad you came," Zeek said as he tried quickly but smoothly to fix himself.

"Should we meet at your home right here, or my place?"

"At your place or in my office?" Zeek nervously asked somewhat confused, while briefly imagining himself conferencing with her in his office. Even

The Perfect Lesson

the thought of her alone with him aroused him further. As he sat there he grew warm and began breathing irregularly, and a mist of perspiration wrapped about his forehead. He took a few deep breaths, disguised as yarns, and exhaled as he wiped his forehead.

When Giz came back into the room he thanked Zeek, but also noticed the bulge in Zeek's pants. With a sneaky smiled he thanked Zeek again and asked Judy, "Are you ready to go, Love?"

Judy looked at Deacon Giz in an interested but unresolved way, then looked back at Zeek, noticing the bulge as well in Zeek's pants, and told him, "I will call you later Deacon Zeek for that appointment and also give you my number. Too bad they took my name off the member's list."

Then she turned back to face Giz, saying, "Well yes! I'm ready, even though I was just getting comfortable!"

Taking her time, she slowly got up and began walking to the door.

Zeek's eyes were glued tightly on every motion, wiggle and wobble of Judy's gluteus, but at the same time instinctively resenting Giz. Zeek stood-up and walked at a comfortable distance for viewing Judy's goods as she left. He stood there briefly in his doorway with his eyes still locked on Judy's fruities in much admiration, and said to himself, 'Damn she's so fine! I know that I'm not suppose to, but I will be waiting for that call Sister Judy!'

Giz looked back at Zeek, and saw that Zeek eyes were still fixed on Judy's fruities.

Giz, with all of his yellowing teeth showing, he smiled, and said, "Ok! See you later, Big Brother!"

Forgive Me Lord

A distraught Deacon Zeek went back into the house, but parted his curtains and watched them as they drove off. He looked down at his pants and saw a wet spot upon his secret area, then felt an overwhelming desire to relieve himself. The thought of Judy kept entering his mind as he slowly went to his bedroom. A voice came to him sounding like his own saying, 'Go ahead, think about her and get it over. Enjoy a few moments. You can't catch anything that way. Once you're done, pray and God will forgive you like he always does. Go ahead. Think about how fat her ass is and about how big her tits are.' Then he thought to himself, 'No, I must be strong. I can't keep doing this everytime I'm over-taken by lust.'

The voice came again saying, 'You even know that famous psychologists, philosophers and athletes can confirm that it's absolutely healthy

The Perfect Lesson

and natural, besides, it will help you to get over her. If you don't, you gonna keep thinking about how fine she is and how bad you really want her. Once you do it, you will be strong again. Look at yourself, your secret is exposed. Go ahead, get some butter and massage it at least.' Zeek began to weaken under the pressure to release and the logic of his lustful cravings.

"Oh boy. Ohhhh. Huhm," he struggled with himself for a few minutes.

Thoughts of Judy kept flooding his mind. He took a handful of cream, invented a dream, got lost in the steam, no shame could be seen while engrossed in the theme of each bubbling scene. Zeek became a prisoner of lust and pleasure as he thought and imagined unlawful intimate fondling with Judy. His total fantasy was all about the hammering the unlawful fruities of Judy's innocent booty. When he had relieved himself, he stood-up feeling whipped and disgraced again by the logic of lust. He went to the bathroom washed his sinful hands and cried out to the Lord. And packing a punch, he struck the wall with his fist, shouting, "Why Lord? Why me?

Why am I having such a hard time with my flesh? I'm a married man. I love my wife and I love you. So why? Oh Lord, please forgive me. I will not do what Giz and my flesh are tempting me to do anymore. I will be strong. I promise this was the last time ever.

I will not commit adultery nor come close to it anymore.

I will seek your face Oh Lord, so please forgive me Lord. I repent right now in the name of Jesus."

Then, that same voice that has been encouraging him to give in over the years, came back to him saying, 'Don't worry, God still love you.

He understands, he knows that you are not perfect, besides you didn't actually commit adultery.'

A guilt ridden Zeek went to bed early without desiring to wait on Ellen. He was still worried about what he may do if he was left alone with Judy or if he were to have that private meeting with her.

The Meeting

Tuesday came to soon for Zeek, for he was still swimming in a sea of guilt. He also has been experiencing difficulty in communicating with Ellen these days, and Ellen was beginning to sense that something was bothering him.

"SweetHeart, I'm leaving," Zeek said as he lingered at the front door before exiting. Ellen dash to the door for a personal goodbye, but by the time she reached the front-door, he was starting the car.

The Perfect Lesson

Ellen mumbled, "Huh. Uhm," and went back to her choirs a little bewildered by this sudden change in mood that she was beginning to observed in Zeek's behavior.

Zeek entered the church from the rear today and took certain backdoor routes to his office, for he did not want to see anyone before getting settled into his office, even-though he was a few hours early. Before he entered his office he noticed Delores standing quietly by the window in the hallway in front of the pastor's office.

She greeted him from a distance with a smile and a nod of the head and looked at the pastor's door, and walked on down the hall. Zeek froze for a spell where he stood, then turned to go where Delores stood. He stood there puzzled for a moment. The hallway was quiet because mostly everyone was out to lunch. Zeek's coat slipped out from his hands just inches from Gateway's door, and as he stooped to pick it up from the floor, he overheard through the cracked opening of the door, Giz saying, "… If you don't believe me ask Judy. Zeek made a smooth move on her Pastor.

He didn't know that I knew that Ella was out visiting the sick. You know the saying Pastor, 'While the cat is away, the mouse will play'."

Zeek stood there in front of the pastor's door holding his coat in shock as he listened in suspense. The more he listened the hotter he became. His gauge was slowly reaching boiling point and approaching the exploding mark, but like Gateway in the park, he could not move. His feet were glued to the floor. He was in a state of suspended animation.

Giz went on: "I know that he's Head Deacon and all, but seriously pastor, this is too much. He really means well, so like we said let's just keep it quiet and maybe he'll repent. He loves women too much. How can you stand in front of one of your sisters in Christ with your thing all hard asking for her phone number? Talkin' bout he wanna private meetin' with her. And he's the Head Deacon——— The Head Deacon!"

The Pastor wrestling to maintain composure asked, "How did you try to steer him in the right direction?"

"Oh! Pastor, you just don't know how hard I tried. Tell you the honest truth Pastor, I done lost track of how many times I tried to steer him in the right direction.

Not only that Pastor, my knees are sore from praying for him and seeking the Lord's face day and night on his behalf.

I don't want nothin' to happen to him, cause me and that boy go way back. But the way he's going, I know Ella gonna find out and its gonna break her poor lil' heart some kind'a bad. Man O'

The Perfect Lesson

man. People don't know Pastor, but me and Zeek is like this…"

After looking around checking to see if anyone was looking, Zeek cautiously peeped thru the cracked door again and saw Giz holding up two fingers fastened together, that suppose to have been symbolizing how tight him and Giz were. For Giz said these things while holding two fingers up stuck together with a serious expression on his face.

In Zeek's silent rage, he imagined himself flinging the door open, busting Giz lip and choking him. Zeek could not take it any more and thought he most control himself or else he would be adding ease dropping and probably hostile charges to his account. So he quietly but swiftly started back to his office while looking back checking to see if he was being watched by someone as he made it down the hall and into his office. He even continued looking behind him as he stuck the key in his office-door, but it was only Delores sympathetically looking at him as if she knew what he was feeling but she continued on her way. Zeek saw her but paid her no mind, he was really looking to see if anyone else had seen him, or was looking. Delores seeing him did not seem to register.

Zeek went into his office and begin to weep sorely and crying, "Oh! Wretched man I am. When shall I be delivered from this body of lust and shame? Why Father? Why God do I keep doing the samething over and over again, even after I pray to you? I just keep doing the same-dang-thing or thinking about doing it. Lord what's wrong with me? Do I have a demon or somethin'? But a demon can't live in a Christian they say. Oh please help me Lord. All of this education I have and I'm still messed-up and missing the mark continually."

Delores also secretly wept, saying, "Lord your Deacons have turned on the other and say they love you." And she continued in secret to pray, intercede and weep.

Zeek was feeling sorry for himself. He felt helpless as if this was his lot in this life and the way he would have to continue to live and die. He also felt like this was some type of thorn. But then for some reason in the mist of all of his plight and troubles, he looked up and saw a great calm and it came over him, then surrounded him and he felt it, and for the first time in his life though all seemed not well he felt relaxed, relieved and as if a huge weight began to be lifted from his shoulders and he said, "Well, here I am Lord! I can't go any lower then this and I can't go back into yesterday. I must be your lowest Deacon and person ever. I should not be even called a Deacon or a Christian. I don't know why Lord, but I feel peace right now in my

The Perfect Lesson

soul. While I'm in trouble and about to lose my office, I feel ok, and when the pastor asks me what did I do? Or did I do what Giz alleged?

I will not add another lie to my account. I will not deny what Giz told him, I will admit that it's all true. I know I shouldn't feel alright right now Lord, but I feel pretty good. I feel like everything is alright eventhough everything is all wrong. Eventhough Deacon Giz turned me in, I feel good right now, but I don't know why. Father God, here I am at the bottom!

Father God, it's not going to help me to hold this against Deacon Giz, so I forgive him too Lord, and again, I am sorry."

Zeek sat there at his desk gazing off, pacing up and down the halls of his mind. Suddenly jolted by some quick successions of knocks on the door, he slowly yet calmly looked at the door and said, "Come in."

When Deacon Giz entered into Zeek's office smiling from ear to ear, Zeek was not surprised.

"Hey! What's up Good Brother?"

"By His grace I believe I'll make it."

"So you doin' well Big Brother?"

"Well as can be expected I guess."

"Know what ya' mean Big Brother. Just thought I would stop by to holler at you."

Zeek answered, "I don't understand this peace, but it's like a river. Excuse me Deacon Giz, I'll be

Young Darby

back." In a sudden hurry, Zeek barreled out the door and up the hall to the pastor's office. Giz was startled but seemed to have ignored this strange behavior and went on to his own office while mumbling to himself under his breath, "He's just as nutty as a gotdamn fruit cake."

"Deacon Zeek, please come in and set down."

"Sorry pastor, but I can't right now."

"What you mean? Have you forgotten our appointment?"

"No sir! I just need some time to prepare for Sunday's service, just in case you want me to say a few words again."

"Do you mean, preach Deacon?" he asked looking into the Deacon's eyes without blinking, but nor did the deacon blink his eyes.

"Well let's just say I want to be ready sir, if you need me."

Gateway stared at the deacon momentarily acknowledging that he have never seen the Deacon looked so at ease and relaxed. But on the other-hand, he also looked something like this on the day that he left the field. His peaceful presence filled the room with such quiet serenity so much that Gateway would not presently consider fully Deacon's Giz allegations concerning Deacon Zeek without giving Zeek another chance to sink or swim.

"See you later by His grace pastor."

The Perfect Lesson

"I'll see you later as well, by his grace also," said the pastor, still staring at Zeek with a very serious and calculating eye as Zeek almost stumbled, backing out of the office.

The pastor sat there with his elbows on his desk and his chin resting on the side of his fist with his thumb wrapped around his chin, wondering what this all meant and what in the world it was going to lead to.

Meanwhile Giz was talking to a long time friend over the phone until he heard whistling in the hallway.

"What? Who in the world..?" said Giz, while almost falling from his chair to look from his doorway to see who it was. When he saw Zeek walking without a care, he repeated, "Who in the world? ...Excuse me, let me call you back, something just came up."

Giz immediately hung-up the phone from talking to his friend and call the pastor.

"Hello! Gateway!"

"Hi Pastor! Have you seen Deacon Zeek yet?"

"Matter-of-fact he just left my office. And by the way, I took your advice about testing him, but he don't know it yet."

"Sir, mind if I ask what kind of test it will be?"

Young Darby

"Well he doesn't know it yet, but at the last minute Sunday coming, he's gonna preach." Giz felt like laughing, but he caught himself, and sat back comfortably in his big chair and said, "Ok pastor, that's good. That will also give him more experience and give him time to reflect on what he's doing."

"I agree Deacon."

"Yes! So that's great pastor. God bless you!"

"And thank you very much for the insight Deacon."

"Anytime Pastor."

"Bye."

"Bye."

Now Giz was on a roll. And he began to plot out his strategy. He decided to call a few long time friends whom he tried several times before to convert to the faith.

"Yo!"

"Hello! Can I speak to Jerry?"

"Yo! Speak'n. Talk to me."

"Hay man this is Giz. How ya' doin'?"

"Hey 'baby boy', wu'd up? I thought you forgot about me since I never join up with ya'."

"Awe man! I was just thinking about you and wanted to ask you if you remembered, Cool Papa from the hood?"

"You talking about the one who was always chasing the chicks and wanted to 'hit-on' my sister that night when I threw the shoe at him, right?"

"That's him."

"Yeah! I remember that faggy!"

"Oh, so you do!"

"Yeah! I remember that no good ass faggit. I didn't tell you man, but he's the reason why I didn't come to your church Cuz, when you kept trying to recruit my black-ass."

"What? I didn't know that."

"Yes-suh dog."

"Why didn't you tell me?"

"Man I wanted to kick his ass 'big time' dog. The more I talked bout it, the more I wanted to pop em'. Know what I'm sayin'?"

"Well aint no need to bring up the reason why I called then."

"Yeah! So wu'd up dog?"

"No!—That's ok!—So how's the crew?"

"Dude, don't even try it! Now what's up? I'm runnin' out of patients now. Why you ask me if I remembered that faggit?"

"Really, that's ok. Now how is the family?"

"You funny man. Ok dog, it's gonna be like that huh?"

"Why you keep calling me dog, dog?"

"Blame! My bad! My bad! My dog. You know sometime I jive be forget'n you're a Deacon and

Young Darby

shit. Oops! I'm sorry again Giz. My bad! My bad! But yo! You can't leave me hangin' like this dude. Wu'd up?"

Deacon Giz took a deep breath and exhaled as if he was forced to give in and said, "Well, your boy, Cool Papa is gonna preach Sunday coming at the 9 o'clock service and I was calling to invite you......"

"What? You shiten me right?"

"Straight up dude. I was just giving you the heads-up buddy and inviting you, plus I'm still trying to get your soul saved. You know what I mean? But if you're still harboring ill feelings...."

"Man I wouldn't miss that for nothin' in the world. I'm gonna come and sit right up in the front freakin' row and be looking right in his big fat lying ass mouth. When he open it up wrong, um gonna jump right up in it, and tell the whole church on his sorry sad low life miserable skirt chasing ass."

"Now you know all that aint necessary Jerry. Why you wanna do that?"

"What y'all call him?"

"Call who?"

"That faggit ass bama!

"Oh! Cool Papa? He's Deacon Zeek now."

"Yeah, ok! I got his deacon."

"So why you wanna be so cold Jerry?"

"He was the one that would always do some dumb shit, then say he's sorry and then go back

The Perfect Lesson

and do the same freakin' thing all over again. Man I can't wait to put my foot up his…"

"Hold it man. Hold it."

"You know how long he's been duckin' me?"

"But hold it Jerry that aint right. That's been years ago. You know God don't like ugly. If you have to say somethin' to him, you can just pull him to the side. He's a reasonable man now, he would understand."

"You don't know em' like I do Deacon."

"He aint all bad. Who knows, this might even be your Sunday."

"It might be his Sunday. And just to wake his memory up I'm gonna bring Ann with me and both of us gonna sit right up front."

"Well if you say so big brother, we'll see you then?"

"Sure thing Giz."

"Ok, but um gonna call you again to remind you Good Brother."

Deacon Giz stood-up brushing the lent off of his suit while posing and admiring himself in the mirror. Then he sat back down and dialed-up Judy.

"Hello"

"Hi…. Judy?"

"Yes it is! Hi Giz!"

"Hi Sweetie, just want to let you know that we have a special surprise guess speaker Sunday and

Young Darby

he request that you come early so you can get a front row seat."

"Who is this guest speaker?"

"Can't tell you that."

"Do he know me?"

"My lips are sealed. I'm under strict orders, besides it would not be a surprise if I told you now, would it?"

"Yeah! You're right. Ok!"

"So ya' comin'?"

"Yeah. I was comin' anyway, but since you told me that, I'm coming early so I can sit up front."

"I knew you was coming anyway. I just wanted to hear your lovely voice."

"Oh you."

"Bye sweetie."

"Thanks for calling Deacon, Bye."

"You welcome dear and don't forget about Saturday prayer meeting."

"I wont. Bye bye!"

"Bye bye!"

After he hung-up, Giz shook his head and said, "Uh uh uh. My my my. Boy I like to hit that."

Then he looked up and said, "But I know I can't Lord so please give me strength cause I'm just a man doing the best I can, but Lord you made that lady so fine. I can just see her now, setting up there on the front row, uh uh uh! Zeek tongue goin' be

The Perfect Lesson

done fell out of his holy ass mouth. Oh! Excuse me Lord! Uh uh uh! Hallelujah!"

Giz sat there shaking his head and started to think about what else he could do to even the score with Zeek to insure that Zeek did not attempt to preach about perfection, and if he did, how could he make him look and feel like a fool and possibly lose his title since he was next in line to be head deacon if Zeek lost his position. So he began to systematically inventory his Rolodex files and make calls.

Meditation

The next day, early in the morning, Zeek left home and drove several miles to the Winding Breeze Park. Only the birds seems to be up at this hour, but not many of them were chirping, for the sun had not cracked the sky yet, though the sun's radiance was radiating arching faint rays of yellows and whites, like beams of search lights upon the navy blue face of the deep.

Zeek walked in the cool of this morning wanting nothing, but what he had at that moment, the stirring gentle winds and the abundance of peace.

Young Darby

He walked silently through the cool of this morning in deep thought. It seemed like only a few minutes went by before the brightest sunrays began to intrude upon the various shaped 'pillo-wee' like clouds and the birds burst forward with a parade of rhythmic tunes. Fragrances of fresh pine filled the air. The musical tune of his watch alerted him that an hour had so soon past and that it was time to go. He reluctantly departed this glorious setting, and it wasn't long before he returned home. Ellen was cooking breakfast as he entered the back door.

"Hi dear! Early morning prayer meeting?"

"Early morning meditation, sweetie," he answered, looking in Ellen's eyes. He paused for a moment, then he went on, "I love you Ella so much. Sometimes I wish life could never end. I wish that we could just live and love each other forever and that we would not have to ever die. I know that I am a Deacon and that I should not be talking like this, because I suppose to understands the stages of life, it's vicissitudes, the inevitable and except the fact that one must reach their end no matter what, and so forth, unless Jesus returns first. But this is how I feel right now baby. And excuse me if I'm sounding kind of irrational, or unreasonable, but sometimes I still wrestle to understand the life span of man and the master's plans. If Ecclesiastic was here, I'm sure he would probably say even my thinking right

The Perfect Lesson

now is vanity and an exercise in chasing the wind, and of this, I'm guilty…."

Ellen, nodding her head in agreement: slowly stretched out her hands, removed a fallen tear hanging from his cheek with a finger and touched his lips saying, "Enough! Your lips are as a morning of fresh dew and your tongue is like a tender peddle that harps on the strings of my heart to the melody of love. I know your pain. I felt the same many times my self, especially at night. There were times I left your side to go and weep alone where you could not see me. And I asked my God why? Why must a true love song die? How come no one is allowed to continue to write his or her song? Why can't Adam and Eve be punished alone for what they've done? Why must we suffer departure? Why should life end anyway? It must be that it is forced to end by design, because I just can't imagine life dying just as I cant imagine death living. And once you're all grown up, it seems the latter part is only for a few more moments? And the days fleet by as if with wings of time: with each flap of the wings equaling a day. Why do we have to leave after we live so long to make some things so right? Yet the longer we live, the shorter we understand life to be.

We build our homes, plan our retirement, finally decorate our walls, and learn to spend wisely. We get the vehicle and earthly home of our dreams: pay-off the mortgage and car notes: learn how to

Young Darby

live reasonably wisely for the most part and then prune our relationships to the fullest and fall so deeply in love as God intended for it to be from the beginning. Then we are forced to prepare to leave. Why give us such a capacity to love and then remove the loved? When we have learned to live and pass all or most of lives quizzes, then we must learn to 'let go' of all. My Lord and my God, please help me to fully understand and accept the things that I cannot change, is my prayer. So dear, you are not alone my most precious and most adorable love. I swear to you: You are not alone."

"Oh my love, don't look at me like that. We will never really be a part. Wherever you are, I will be," said Zeek.

Ellen replied, "Wherever you are, I will be also."

Zeek looked at his wife and held her in his arms and they softly wept together for the samething at the same time, as they have not done, in such a long time, about something they still did not understand. They only knew that they felt the same. And Zeek took all of these things to heart. They decided today that they would cancel all plans and appointments. They placed the phone on auto-answer-mode and stayed home talking, sharing and reading scriptures.

The Perfect Lesson

The phone seemed to have been ranging louder than ever the next morning. Ellen was already up, but Zeek reached over and answered the phone.

"Hello! Hello!"

"Hey Big Brother! You still sleepin'?"

"What time is it?" Zeek asked while stretching and yarning.

"It's day time fool," Giz shot.

"What?" Zeek said, being a little disturbed by Giz calling him a fool.

"Man it's almost noon. What you been doing?"

"Sleepin', what ya' think?"

"I know you comin' in today. We're all here. Did Ella bake that germen chocolate cake?"

"Yeah! I think so."

"Ok Big Brother! See you when you get here."

"Ok."

Zeek hung-up and asked Ellen, "Baby did you know that you suppose to make a cake for the missionary meeting today?"

Ellen stopped in her tracks, dashed to the kitchen and started popping her fingers and began grabbing bowls, flour and all she needed to bake the cake.

"Baby I know ya' not gonna try to make the cake right now are ya'?"

"Just watch me! It slipped my mind——I'll whip it up, put it in the oven and you can run back here and pick it up in about 55minutes, she hollered."

"Huh!"

"Yeah! Time everybody finish eatin' the food, it'll be ready."

"Ok!" said Zeek as he made himself ready.

Thursday's Missionary Meeting

At the church there was much talking in private and in open discussions, and much laughter. Everyone seems to be very happy as they made the food ready and participated in open fellowship in the church's fellowship hall.

After casually looking around, Deacon Giz smoothly slipped out of a side-door without being noticed and headed straight for his car. He drove a few blocks from the church till he found a nice quiet area along side a huge shade-giving tree and parked. He turned on his radio, set-up his cup, pulled out his favorite appetizer: Harvey's Bristol Cream, and started to take slow swigs. This is something he always liked doing during meals and before he ate, as an appetizer, especially more-so when there was a party.

He couldn't find anything kicking on the radio, as he surfed the radio-bands, so he popped in one of his oldies but goodies: 'Flash Light', and began

The Perfect Lesson

to groove and dance in his seat and sipping at the same time. Man, he was feeling some kind-of good.

In the meanwhile, Zeek had done rushed out of the house and was on his way. On his way to church, he decided to take a few shortcuts, which put him on a certain back street.

As the street began to twist and wind around a certain corner, he noticed a familiar looking parked car that seems to have been slightly bouncing. Zeek could not seem to take his eyes off of the bouncing car, because it looked so familiar.

As he drew closing, he observed a head bobbin up and down, saw arms jerking and fingers popping to music, and smoke coming from the car windows. As he got even closer to the car, he heard the music more clearer: with his mouth slightly open, he cautiously drove along side the car, and to his amazement he could not believe that it was Deacon Giz taking a slow drag off of a cigarette, while holding a bottle in the other hand, pouring a drink. Without thinking Zeek shouted, "Deacon Giz? Hey what you doing man? What in the…"

Giz immediately lunged forward in surprise and when he turned his head to see who shouted, his cigarette fell out from his hand down between his legs and the fire from it burned a hole in his paints

Young Darby

and rolled down between his legs onto the car seat and his drink in his other hand poured onto his shirt and lap. Giz began frantically beating between his legs to put out the fire.

"Gotdam-it! Shit man," he said as he frantically scrambled from the car while he continued to beat his paints and the smoking driver's seat, while hatefully looking over at Zeek.

Again Zeek went, "What in the…"

Then in troubling silence, Zeek paused, looking confused, then asked: "Brother Giz, what ya' doin' out here?"

"Man, kiss my brotherly ass."

"Huh."

"What ya' doing spying on me like that?"

"Spying on you?"

"Yeah! Dam'it! See what you done did?"

"Aint no body spying on you brother. I was just on my way in, and couldn't but help notice somebody dancing in the car and the smoke fumes."

"Dancing and smoke fumes my ass! You mean to tell me you never saw smoke fumes?"

Zeek sat there with his mouth open, looking at Giz.

"You never smoked?"

"Well yeah."

"Your momma never smoked?"

"What?"

"You never saw anybody smoking before?"

The Perfect Lesson

"But..."

"Man don't even try that shit with me," Giz said as he climbed back into his car wiping off his shirt, paints and shoes.

"I'm sorry for scaring you like that. But man, why are you out here drinking and smoking like this?"

Giz was so hot, he didn't even respond this time.

"I thought you stopped drinkin' and smokin' along time ago."

"Once in a while I still like to take a little drink for an appetizer just before I eat something. It enhances the flavor. Ok? I forgot you never tried it!"

"Awe man!"

"You do know, the Bible 'doesn't' say we can't drink don't you?"

"Well..."

"Matter-of-fact, one of the first miracles Jesus did was to turn water into wine. You do remember that don't you?"

"Yeah! I know..."

"And the scripture said the wine that Jesus made was better then the wine that they was drinking at first, shit."

"Yeah! But you must remember, the things written in the bible was written to teach us lessons and for examples in righteousness."

Young Darby

"Ok! So now you want to start preachin' to me cause you caught me drinking a little appetizer. Right?"

"No um just…"

"I didn't preach to you when you was looking at Judy fat ass and tits, did I?"

"I repented of that and of everything that I've done wrong. You know…"

"Oh, really?"

"Well anyway, I done made up my mind to serve the Lord with my whole heart."

"Since when?"

Zeek paused and continued: "Don't worry I'm not goin' to tell on you."

Infuriated, Giz shouted, "What? You think I'm worried about you telling on me?"

"I'm just sayin'."

"I'm just sayin' too: boy, I'll put all your shit in the street. Think you holier than thou, do you? Aint you the sameone that was foaming at the mouth talking to the missionary the other-day in your very own house, with your dick all hard and shit?"

"What?"

"Yeah! That's right. I saw you."

"Huh," Zeek said in surprise, with his mouth hung opened.

"Got news for you Big Brother, she saw your perfect ass too."

"Now Brother Giz!"

The Perfect Lesson

"Brother my ass! You can play up to the pastor ass all you want, but remember; I know your sneaky ass. I knew you before you started going to church. Shit, if it weren't for me, you wouldn't even be up in the joint. Head Deacon my ass."

"What's up with you, Giz? Why all the attitude?"

"Yeah! Uh-huh, and I know you still wanna try to preach that 'perfect' shit, but if you do, I'm gonna be setting right there just like I was the last time. I'll be like white on yo' rice, but with brother Jerry and the crew this time. I'm gonna have something for your holy ass when you finish. Talkin' bout you aint gonna tell on me."

Zeek mouth fell open even wider, and he began to wipe his mouth and rub his chin in utter disgust. He looked in his rear-view mirror observing a developing car line that was growing behind him and becoming impatient as they honked their horns. Some of the cars honked as they eased passed him and other yelled out for him to move. Without replying to Giz, Zeek gave him the 'stern eye' and drove off.

"What's that suppose to mean? I know you aint tryin' do nothin', with your phony-ass-self," Giz yelled, as Zeek drove off.

Young Darby

Giz set there for a few more minutes muttering under his breathe, "That Sum-o-bitch been not say nothing. I'll put all his shit in the street." Giz paused, to get himself together while shaking his head and said, "Lord please forgive me. Dag! Lord next week, I'm gonna pray and fast the whole week long and read too. He made me mad Lord. I don't like using words like that. Please forgive me in the name of Jesus. Amen."

Then he took the scope out of the glove compartment, goggled several times, cracked opened the door, expelled and drove off.

Zeek was at his boiling point as he pulled into his parking spot at the church. He sat there briefly speaking the word of God to himself to calm himself down:

"Greater is he that is in me than he who is in the world. I can do all things through Christ who strengthen me. No weapons formed against me shall prosper. If they persecuted Jesus they shall also persecute me. I am not better then my Lord. If they accept Jesus, they will also accept me.

If they rejected Jesus, they gonna reject me too. I will not be weary in well doing. If I feint in the time of adversary my strength is little. When I am weak, then I am strong. Jesus said that he would be

The Perfect Lesson

with me even until the end of the world. Victory is mines. Also trials, testing, tribulations, death, life, poverty as well as prosperity are mines. In the end I shall come fourth as pure gold, even now. I must be perfect even as my father in heaven is also perfect."

When Zeek stepped out of the car, he heard the heavens rumbled from a far with the sounds of a distant thunder. As he walked up the staircase, it quickly, showered a brief drizzle. He then mounted his way up the stairs quickly while covering his head with his Bible and once he entered thru the church glass doors and looked back outside and up at the sky, he observed that just that quick, it had stopped raining. The sky looked calm and clear and the most beautiful of all rainbows appeared, seemingly from one end of the earth to the other while arching thru the highest clouds. The pink, yellow, green, orange, blue and purple brilliant colors were in true hues of awe. Zeek seemed to be momentarily hypnotized as he looked on at this magnificent brilliant arching rainbow. Suddenly he felt something move within him and sensed an awakening in himself.

As he walked to his office, tears filled his eyes and he had no control over what was happening as his chest heaved from the pressure to force him

Young Darby

to emote. He could not make himself stop and he tried earnestly not to be seen. He cried even with his voice and a few ushers saw him but only looked at eachother as if to say, 'I don't know why!' When Delores saw him fighting back the tears she warmly handed him her napkin but asking him nothing, and placed her hand on his back, petting him, and walked with him to his office: took the keys from his hand, open his door, handed him his keys back and he walked into his office alone and she closed his door, tugged up her skirt, straightening her skirt back out and left him, not asking a single question.

The Perfect Lesson

Chapter 9
He called me a Jackass!

When Deacon Giz reached the church, the aroma of chicken, yams, greens and pig-feet, fish and hot country buttered biscuits heartily lured him straight to the hall where the food was being prepared and served. He peeped in but did not go inside. He managed again to slip by folk and made it to his office where he changed his clothes, brushed his teeth, and tidy-up before entering the fellowship hall. Once he reentered the hall, it seemed as if he have forgotten about everything that just took place as he grabbed a spoon and plate, dug in and began to feast. He began to mingle and laugh with others and was quite merry. Shirley went forward and made the scheduled announcements about the upcoming events, and for the first time Delores also made an announcement: "Please hold Deacon York in prayer. Eventhough the pastor will be here this Sunday, Deacon York will be the speaker bringing fourth a special word from our Lord and Savior Jesus Christ. Thank You!"

"When Giz heard that, he asked, "Where is Deacon Zeek by the way?"

One of the ushers that were standing nearby who saw him in the hallway said, "We saw him

Young Darby

with Sister Delores. She was really holding on to him and went with him into his office."

Deacon Giz, Grin and said, "What? He don't waste no time. That rascal is at it again. He aint change for nothing. Um um um. Thanks for telling me."

A bit surprised by the Deacon response, the usher hesitated to go, and while slightly smiling and lingering, asked, "Why did you say that Deacon?"

"Well let's just say that our good Deacon has some unresolved issues with anything with a skirt these days," Deacon Giz readily responded, "but you didn't hear that from me sister."

The usher put her hand to her mouth and looked at her friend who was standing close by who also heard what Deacon Giz had said. They both went off discussing it, and eventually among themselves, accusing Delores of fraternizing as the conversation grew with a few others. As the ushers walked off, with food still in Giz's mouth, Giz hollered out, "One of you sisters tell Deacon Zeek to come on down. It's not fair. These ladies worked to hard to let all of this delicious food go to waste," he said while still chewing.

"Yes sir Deak!" the ushers quipped.

But before they could get to his office, Deacon Zeek was on his way to the feast.

The Perfect Lesson

"How are my precious sisters doing today?" he asked as he greeted the ushers. "Y'all didn't eat up all the food yet, did you?"

"Oh no! It's plenty. By-the-way, Deacon Giz is looking for you," one of the ushers told him. He thanked her and went on. When he entered the fellowship hall, he saw a host of members and friends talking and dining. Some setting, some standing and in a far corner he saw Deacon Giz, Shirley and Judy talking as if they were having a major conference.

Shirley noticed that Zeek was coming, so she stood-up and immediately approached him and greeted him as he began to draw nearer along the isle where they sat.

She welcomed him with a loving hug and a kiss to the jaw. Zeek modestly smiled and welcomed here to sit with him at a near by vacant spot. As they sat and chat, Zeek poised questions to Shirley regarding her ideas of the ideal marriage.

A waiter came and served them and they sat, talked and ate. Shortly afterwards Zeek excused himself to run home to pick up the cake that his wife was making. When he left, Giz came over and began to make a small stir, whispering to Shirley, saying, "Deacon still got the 'hots' for you don't he Shirley?"

"Oh no he don't. He was just asking for my opinion about what I thought the ideal marriage should be like."

"Boy I tell you, you got to give it to him. He's one smooth dude aint he?"

"Huh!" Shirley said.

Deacon Giz slid over closer alongside Shirley, stood-up, shook his head, looking down at her while he was standing like he did not know what to say. Then he gestured like he was going to speak, but did not, shook his head again and with his most sincerest expression, looked at Shirley saying, "Shirley can I tell you something?"

"Sure Deacon."

"But first you got to promise me that you will keep all that I'm about to tell you to yourself."

Shirley eyes and ears were foaming with anticipation as she innocently replied, "Oh! Who would I tell? You know I could keep stuff."

Giz sat down and continued, "That Damn Deacon Zeek aint nothing but a snake in the grass."

Shirley's eyebrows leaped to the ceiling as her eyes squinted to listen.

"I know you wonder why I been calling you so much lately. But it was for him. He had me doing his undercover work to feel you out. You know, something told me something was wrong, because I prayed and prayed about that thing and the Lord told me just as clear as day, 'Go ye and tell him to

The Perfect Lesson

repent.' But I admit, I disobeyed the Lord thinking that I was helping Deacon Zeek."

Shirley jumped in, "But what do you mean? Do you mean that day when you said when he see me he don't wanna sit down?"

Giz took a deep breath and nodded yes with his head, and said, "Shirley! You know what that snake told me?"

"What?"

"He said everytime he see you his 'Johnson' jump straight up in the air and he have to sat down to hide it."

Shirley head snapped back, and she began choking, gagging and coughing from the string beans that she was already chewing quite rapidly while eagerly listening. Something must have gone down the wrong pipe. She tried to cover her mouth but for a moment could not stop coughing.

Giz was gladly holding her and petting her and rubbing her back. Finally she recovered saying: "Oh my goodness! Oh! My God! Deacon what's wrong with that man?"

"I don't know. Don't get me lying!"

"Now he can't be going around saying things like that, he' suppose to be a happily married man.

At least that's the way he's been acting, plus he's the head deacon. He suppose to be an example. Oh my Lord Jesus! Are you sure?"

Young Darby

"Don't let that humble act fool you sister! He got some problems believe it or not. But the thing that really got me was when sister Judy and me stopped by his house last week. He almost went to pieces trying to peep down her bosoms and trying to get some play. He couldn't take one eye off of her bosom, and told her he had some important business to discuss with her in private. Afterwards he called me and said he didn't know which one he wanted the most between you and Judy. Then he grinned and said if he met you two in Africa he'll take all both of your fat asses."

"Deacon, are you serious?"

"Here's my hand!"

Shirley became speechless.

"Now what really took the cake is this. A few days ago he told me there was someone special and meek here and that if he could get with that certain person, he would give all y'all up."

"What he mean by that? He don't have me!"

Giz paused and began rubbing his chin like he was reluctantly telling on Zeek. Then he continued in a quieter voice, while peeping around to make sure no one was looking or listening saying, "Now, he did not tell me who this special someone was, but I stepped out today and when I returned, Zeek had already gotten here, and Sister Cathy said she saw Delores coming from Deacon Zeek's office tucking in her blouse and pulling up her skirt. What that sound like?"

Shirley put her hand over her mouth and said, "Oh my God."

Now you know I'm not gonna lie on sister Cathy! And if you don't believe me, she's setting right over there. Go ahead ask her!"

"Oh my God Deacon Giz! I heard enough. Poor old Ella! I knew something was wrong. I know it."

"Like what?"

"Well the way he preached that short message last time, I just felt like something wasn't right."

Shirley thought back again about his last sermon and remembered seeing him looking at her legs a few times as he struggled to get himself together. Shirley blurted out, "Maybe that's why he said, 'Help me, and pray for me'. And, 'I m coming.'"

"What?" Giz did not understand.

"Oh nothing. Well thanks Giz, but don't you think, you or the pastor need to go and talk and pray with him before this thing get out of hand and somebody get hurt?"

"Shirley baby, I tried the best I could, and I'm done with him. I told him earlier today if he didn't straighten-up, I'm finish with him.

I'm just gonna put him in the Lord hands. I'm gonna forgive'em and just let the Lord handle him so my conscious can be clear, and ask the Lord to have mercy on him. That's all I can do. It just makes

Young Darby

me mad when somebody just keep on sinning, especially a deacon. You know what I mean?"

"Uhm hum! You are a good man Deacon Giz."

"I try. Cause I'm gonna see Jesus one day, and I want to be right. You know what I mean?"

"I sure do. Why did you get divorced anyway?"

"I'll just say this. If you don't want to do what the Lord say and honor his holy word, I aint got time for you. See I don't hang out and do those foolish things I use to do. I admit I'm not perfect but there's certain things you not suppose to do when you call yourself walkin' in the Master's footsteps." With his most sincerest and honest face he continued, "You see, that's the other reason why Zeek is mad with me, because I told him that I really thought you was the sweetest women I ever met and that you deserve the very best."

Shirley shyly bowed her head down and began blushing, and replied, "Oh, Deacon you are so sweet yourself to say that."

"Thank you baby."

The Hall Room Brawl

Zeek made it back with the germen chocolate cake dashing thru the door calling out: "One Hot Germen Chocolate Cake coming up." With a kind look, he greeted mostly everyone he encountered and took the cake to the kitchen, smiling and

The Perfect Lesson

causally waving at Shirley as he walked past them. At this point, the mere sight of Zeek tended to trigger resentment and ill feelings in Giz. This afternoon, when Zeek walked passed Giz, Giz seemed to have been jolted with resentment at the very sight of Zeek, but managed to force a slight smirk of a smile for the sake of Shirley and everybody else that may have been looking.

When Zeek walked along the area where Shirley and Giz were now seated, he stopped, smiled and said: "You're ok Shirley?"

Shirley looking down at the table, said, "I'm fine, I guess, by his grace." Then she popped her head up to actually look at him as he stood there with that broad smile on his face, "And you Deacon Zeek? You look like you worked-up a sweat."

"Oh sister Shirley, I've never been better. I'm born again! And the Lord has forgiven me of all of my sins."

In an accepting way, Shirley nodded and glanced at Giz. Deacon Giz, feeling Shirley eyes, but without exchanging Shirley's glance, stood-up, put one hand on his waist, grasping the opportunity to score, saying, "I thought you was already born again, Big Brother! You mean to say you been 'playing Deacon' all this time? Well excuse me!" Giz gritted as if he were only teasing, sat back down, and began patting on the table with his fingers. A

Young Darby

few members heard it and laughed, taking it as an innocent joke in the spirit of good times.

"Ha..ha..ha!" Zeek sniggled and laughed along with the members and replied, "That's a good one! You got me! You got me! But believe me Giz, you aught to try it yourself. It'll make you feel real good."

Now the members looked at Giz and began laughing at him even harder. The 'Ha…ha…haws' and 'He…he..hees', were bubbling along their table.

"Um born again buddy and don't have to brag about it, cause I know it."

"You could have fooled me Little Brother," Zeek said with two fingers flush to his lips like he was smoking.

Taken offence, Giz rose up from his chair, but this time looking a little serious, "What you mean by that?"

Zeek replied, "I meant what I said. You aught to try being born again yourself my Little Brother."

The members that heard this comment put their hands over their mouth and made funny stares at each other, saying, "Wooo…," and "Ooopps."

Now, Giz tried his best not to show it, but grew increasingly infuriated, to the point that a nerve in his jaws twitched and he did not really care who heard him at this point. It was as if the devil momentarily took over: "Man who in the world

The Perfect Lesson

you think you are?" Sensing the mounting tension, Shirley grabbed Giz free arm, encouraging him to set back down and stop: "Deacon Giz please calm down. He didn't mean anything by it. I'm sure! Did you Deacon Zeek?"

Zeek smiled at Shirley, shook his head and walked away with a plate of food in his hand and headed on to his office, saying, "I'm out of here. He can dish it out but can't take it."

"I can handle anything you got," shot Giz.

"Oh yeah?" Zeek questioned as he turned back around and placed his plate on the table.

"Yes I can! What you got Zeek? What you got?" Giz barked as he aggressively advanced towards Zeek. A few of the other deacons seated nearby came over between them speaking to them to calm them down. But the whole hall was in an up-roar by now as they witnessed and debated the Deacons brief standoff.

Every table was filled with questions about what happen, who started it, and how it was so out of place for Christians to argue, especially in the church. Yet, Deacon Giz yelled out again at Deacon Zeek while Zeek was leaving the hall: "And you know God don't' like adulterers, Deacon."

Zeek countered, "God don't like Jack asses either."

"What? Now did y'all hear what he call me?"

Young Darby

The hall was filled with excitement and wonder as many tried to tame the situation before Gateway came.

Shirley whispered to Giz, "Oh my goodness. I thought you said he was just talking about it? You didn't say that he actually did anything."

Deacon Giz replied without lowering his voice, "Its' the samething in God's sight. If you think it, it's just like doing it in God's sight, that's what my bible says."

"Well excuse me! Let me go check things out in the kitchen," Shirley said as she casually and politely got up from this heated table of attention, and faded away into the kitchen. But when she reached a quiet corner in the kitchen, it wasn't long before many busy bodies surrounded her, questioning her on what happened at her table and who started the fight.

Later that evening when Zeek got home, as he paced up and down the floor, he could not wait for Ellen to come so he could tell her about what went on at church as he could not stop pacing up and down the floor. He kept running the scene of what happen at church over and over again in his mind. Every-time he tried to think of something

The Perfect Lesson

else, it kept coming back as if his mind was on auto rewind.

Finally he calmed down and took a tall cold coke from the refrigerator, parked in front of the tube reclining in his easy-boy while reflecting, then began navigating the tube with his remote while nodding between swigs and sips of the coke until he found his favorite news station. Before he could finish his drink, Ellen came.

"Hi Sweetie! Wake-up. If I was a burglar, you would have been wasted," Ellen kidded.

"Oh! Hi baby! How was your day?" Zeek replied halfway yarning and stretching.

"My day was wonderfully blessed, how 'bout yours?"

"I'll wait till you settle-down because you aint gonna believe what I been thru today."

"I know it wasn't that bad!"

"That's what you think!"

"Ok! Just wait one minute, let me put my things down."

She hurried and put her bags, and coat down and eagerly approach the sofa to learn about the commotion that went on today at church. She couldn't wait to hear every ungodly detail of what happened and Zeek could not wait to start talking.

"Baby I don't know how I'm going to preach on Sunday. I hope the pastor call somebody else or preach himself."

Young Darby

"Now hold it right there 'Baby'! What happen today?"

Zeek began to tell all that happened, starting at the part about where he saw Giz on the roadside not far from the church getting twisted, completely thru their fall-out at church, not leaving anything out. Ellen was flabbergasted, for she had nothing but the highest regards for Deacon Giz, and it was obvious that a part of her still did not want to believe it for the sake of the gospel and her Christian relationship with Giz. As Zeek continued he also shared some of his personal secrets regarding past 'flames' in his life and some terrible indiscretions even among church flames which he had repented of as well as other experiences he had with Giz, in which he referred to as, 'back in the days', when Giz was called 'Rags' and himself was called, 'Cool Papa'.

For in those days, they both dressed so well that certain department store managers styled and coordinated the garments and color pattern of their manikins after their eye-catching appeal and postures and no lady, young or old, would pass by them without looking atleast twice. They were also called the 'dressers'. Some say that this is how the Ragtime era got its name.

Ellen looked into her husband softly set sorrowful eyes, took his hands and began to pray for strength and peace in his spirit, then quietly asked, "What time are you going in tomorrow?"

The Perfect Lesson

"I don't think I'm goin' in tomorrow baby! I think I'll just stay home, study, seek the Lord's face and take it easy. They sat quietly and reflected on their day and turned in around 12:45am before Zeek dosed off.

[Friday]

It was 5am and the phone began to ring, flooding out all peace and quiet, and Ellen's idea of covering her ears with pillows, just didn't work. Ellen began shoving Zeek to wakeup and answer the phone but he was snoring so hard she gave up.

Finally it stopped ringing but minutes later it started back again.

"Yes! Hello?" Ellen finally answered.

"Hi Sis Ella! This Brother York. I know it's early, but I need to speak with Deacon Zeek, It's about Shirley's brother."

"What's wrong with him?"

"He's in Freedman's. He just went into a coma."

"Oh my Lord."

"The pastor told me to call."

"Where's the pastor?"

"He's still in Jersey."

"Ok. Oh my goodness! Zeek, wake-up," Ellen cried out while briskly shaking him.

"Here, this is Brother York. Deacon Marcus is in a coma," she said handing him the phone.

Young Darby

"What?" Zeek snapped from his heavy snoring, as if he was already awake, saying: "Mighty man Mark!"

"Yeah, here, talk to'em."

Zeek grabbed the phone: "What hospital is he in?"

"Shirley said he's in Freedman."

"What room?"

"He's in IU."

"Where is Sister Shirley?"

"She's over there."

"Did you call Deacon Giz?"

"Yeah! I called him about five times, but his answering machine kept coming on. But I left several messages on his machine."

"Ok buddy, I'm on my way. Bye."

Zeek hurriedly threw a shirt and pair of paints on, stuck his feet in some shoes without looking, without socks, grabbed his keys, kissed Ellen and dashed out the house.

"Drive carefully sweetie," Ellen warned.

While on his way, Zeek began to ask God and himself many questions.

With shallow breath and tons of nervous energy rushing thru him, Zeek asked, "What am I gonna do? Lord, do you want me to just pray over him? Are you going to heal him Lord? Lord do I really need to go, because I can pray for him at home and you can heal from anywhere. You can even heal

The Perfect Lesson

him while I'm on my way, and some one could call me before I get there. And Lord, Mighty Mark is a good man, full of life, and truth. Why did this had to happen to him anyway? I know Mark Lord. He's good. He may not be perfect but he's good Lord. He's closer to perfection then me. You know how he is, his walk, his humbleness, his eagerness to help anybody at anytime, his unselfishness, his visiting the sick, the shut in, the jails he visits, the lame the insane and the way he seem to understand and know their hurt without even questioning you Lord. He even have away of feeling people pain in his legs wherever they maybe hurting in their body. He never even question you Lord, at least I never heard him question you Lord. He accepted your word of perfection more readily then me. He seems to unconditionally believe in you Lord. So Lord why did you let this happen to him? And why are you sending me?

"He is better then me. He always was. He always will be because that's the way you made him and I am glad and am not even a little a shame. I love him and know that you love him more than I do, and more then I can, but do you have to let him go thru all of this?"

Zeek paused while momentarily sobbing then continued making his case before the Lord with tears and groaning, Father God I don't know why you are allowing this: but I know in my heart you

Young Darby

are in control of this: of pulling people thru, is what I seen you do, so from the bottom of my heart, I must confess, Oh' enemy of God with you I'm not impressed. These blows you throwing at my buddy will have no effect: but will make him be a soldier in the face of death. Sickness and disease and things that knock you to your knees, In my God's presents um sayin' they're no contest: so move me thru the press got to see him pass this test and see my God's hand, moving all thru this mess: in Jesus name, my Lord, you are the very best.

When Zeek reached the hospital, the clerk at the information desk directed him to IU. When he entered the IU room where Mark was, he saw Shirley crying by Mark bedside. Mark was attached to life-supports with a number of wires connected. Zeek tried not to count or see all the wires, but his eyes were on auto count. Every wire he saw seemed numbered. Bent Mike was also there seated on the other-side of the bed with a look of renewal on his face as he gladly and humbly greeted Deacon Zeek. Shirley also greeted Deacon Zeek but he did not verbally speak back to her, instead nodded as he did at bent Mike. The Deacon softly asked Shirley to stand outside of the room while he spoke with Mark, but she refused and cried even more to the point that bent Mike had to use many kind words and gentle persuasion to pry her out of the room.

The Perfect Lesson

Deacon Zeek shook his head in sorrow, and looked up to the Lord and said, "Lord they called upon the elders of the church, and one elder is here requesting a reprieve for our brother Mark's life."

He then looked at Mark and saw no sign of Life, but only the sounds of a heaving respirator, beeping devices and gadgets which drove him instantly into indignation as he screamed out, "Mighty Man Markus Get Up from this stuff right now.

I command you in the name of Jesus Christ, even by his power that is at work in me! Get up!"

He shouted so loud some nurses in the hall and in the next room also shouted by reflex.

Someone dropped their clipboard at the nurse's station. A doctor in the hallway farted, realizing what he'd done, put his hand over his mouth. Several nurses and staff members tore into the room and found Mark setting-up asking, "What's wrong?"

Seeing that Mark was setting up and wide awake, the staff members asked, "What happened?"

"How long have I been here? What happened Deacon Zeek? Man I'm hungry," Mark continued.

Zeek was still on fire and in a holy ghost rage in his 'spirit-man' and found it difficult holding his peace as he commanded the staff members that entered the room to bring food and unhook Mark from the machines. They all were perplexed and excited, but they urged the Deacon to please step outside of the room so they could examine the patient. But Zeek said, "The patient is well and hungry, disconnect him and bring him something to eat". Annoyed by the deacon, the staff began to demand that he leave the room, saying that the patient may be in shock, which could make things even worst at this point. Reluctantly Deacon Zeek stepped out, but as he made his way out, Shirley and bent Mike pressed by him to enter in, for the medical staff recognized them as direct family members, and when they saw Mark setting up, alert, and in his right mind, they started praising God and began to explain to the staff members who Deacon Zeek was and how close the Deacon is with the Lord. None of the doctors or nurses paid them much attention or seemed to have even cared about what they said, but continued to attend to their medical devices, and reading and recording Mark's vital signs.

After praising God and sharing their joy with Mark for a very short while, Bent Mike and Shirley were also ordered to step-out of the room so that the physician and nurses could complete their examination.

When they went out to the waiting area to wait till the staff complete their examination, they looked around for Deacon Zeek to thank him, but he was no where to be found, for he was on his way back home. By this time, he was driving along the way

The Perfect Lesson

enjoying the magnificent hues of the sun's whites, orange and red rays as they penetrated the vast blue yonder, and Zeek praised God all the way home and prayed that God should purge him right then and keep him purged and fit to do the master's work.

Ellen was waiting. When he entered, she had a light breakfast already prepared for him. After entering the house, she stopped him with baited breath asking him, "Dear, how did he look? You think he will be OK?"

Zeek looked at Ellen, stretched forth his hands, saying, "Baby, it happen' again!"

Ellen stood frozen. Zeek continued, "The Lord healed him before my very eyes. My very own eyes! I must admit that I was a little confused and perhaps a little hot with the Lord on my way over-there.

But when I was praying I got so mad at the devil until I hated the devil more then ever before. I mean it. I hate him. Even now, I hate him."

"Sweet heart, I believe that God is going to use you in a mighty way. I believe that this is just the beginning."

"Come on baby, he's already using me. And this morning I discovered that it is easier to talk to someone than it is to pray for someone, and it is easier to say a simple prayer for someone than

Young Darby

it is to command that they be healed. Boy, it is so much easier to say, 'be blessed and go in peace'. Commanding that someone be healed, delivered, or to rise, is hard work done by the inner-man. It's draining, taxing and exhausting...... Baby after I eat please hold all my calls, because I'm going into my prayer closet. I got to sought some things out."

"Ok! Sweetheart," Ellen said as she went back to her choirs.

Zeek prayed and studied without ceasing throughout that day or until sunset.

Meanwhile, before evening, the word had spread to the church that Deacon Zeek healed brother Mark. In a side-bar meeting in the church parking lot, Deacon Giz was expressing how much he resented it by the way he spoke to a group of fellow deacons at a staff meeting, saying, "What's wrong with folk? Don't people know that God is the healer and not man? Man can't do anything. God was going to heal him anyway. Now here he is getting all the credit for what God did, like he did it, and not God. I could have went and prayed for him and he still would've gotten better. Then they would be saying that I did it. And a matter-of-fact, I was praying for brother Mark too. A good thing

The Perfect Lesson

I wasn't praying in the open, cause then some will be saying, I healed him.

People better be careful on who they lift up and give praise to!"

This brought on a slight dissension in the church, because some wanted to recognize and give Deacon Zeek some recognition and some wanted to give all recognition and praise to God without recognizing Zeek as having anything to do with it.

[Saturday]

Deacon Zeek rose early and went to the field where it all began, and where all things at first made since. Quietly he walked up and down the grassy field pondering over the pastor's remarks regarding perfection and God's will. He soon stopped pacing, looked upward and broke the silence of this gleaming morning still filled with glistening stars, and said, "Lord, I know that at my best I'm still only clay, but Lord I dare you to allow me to bury all of my fears out here today, right now, and follow you with my whole heart and audibly promise me, Zeek, that you got my back whatever, what so-ever-ever. If you do this Lord, I will purpose to be perfect and will walk in lion's dens. I will thread on the heads of scorpions.

I will run and not get weary. I will praise your name in the presents of demonic forces, witches, and warlocks and command their destinies. I will be a real follower of Jesus Christ and no weapon formed against me shall have a possibility of prospering unless you give it permission. Lord you want me perfect? I want to be perfect! Let's agree on it right now Lord and settle this thing forever. What you say Lord? ....Deal?"

Zeek stood around eagerly awaiting a response.

After about a half an hour of waiting he went over and stood where he prayed, but did not hear anything, but he did leave that place feeling strong and refreshed. As he drove-off, he could not help notice that he felt more stronger in his faith and in his body than he have ever felt at any point in his life. He began to make sounds with his mouth to check his voice and to look at himself in the mirror as if he knew something was changed but he still looked the same, but his faith was as a burning flame and he felt as if he could turn his car over or pull a steal door off from it's hinges.

He could not wait to reach home. But when he did, he made his way straight to the bathroom, took off his shirt to look at his newly felt muscular definition, but to his amazement there was no change: no new definition in muscle tone, no new muscular physical features.

He walked around the house flexing his triceps, then went back to the mirror, steal no change in appearance nor have he heard anything audibly

The Perfect Lesson

from the Lord yet. Ellen notice the irregular activity and movement that Zeek was making from where she stood in the house, and called out, "Dear? You Ok?"

"Yeah baby, I'm fine."

"You need anything before I go to the store?"

"No baby, I'm Ok," he said as he flexed his muscles in the mirror looking for some hidden muscular features and signs of newly forming definition anywhere.

"Ok! Breakfast is on the oven," she hollered.

"Thanks Baby. But don't forget, no breakfast for me tomorrow," he said as he continued to look for an outward sign that he was definitely stronger.

He looked at himself from his head to his toe but could not find any clues.

Finally he gave up. He went to the kitchen, brought his food before the tube, said his grace, set back in his favorite chair and all of a sudden he heard a voice calling, crystal clear, "Zeek!"

Zeek became frozen, then slowly looked around. Thinking it was in his head, he leaned back again. Again he heard his name being called, "Zeek!" This time Zeek stood-up as if he was being watched and said, "Who is that?"

For this time, the voice was so near and audible, he checked the bathroom, peeped out his front window, and even looked inside of the bedroom under the bed, and in the closet. Finally he called

Young Darby

out to Ellen to see if she had come back home yet or maybe she did not leave and was still in the house. But after surveying the house, he confirmed that no one was there but him. He became quiet again, and listen, but this time heard nothing.

So he put his food back on his lap and began to devour a spoonful, but before the spoon could enter his mouth, he heard the voice, saying, "I am with you even until the end of the world, and let the weak say they are strong."

Zeek immediately turned to see who spoke, but saw no one. Seeing that no one was around him spoke these words for sure, and acknowledging the fact that Ellen was gone, Zeek shouted, "Halleluiah. Praise the Lord. Is that you Lord? Thank you Jesus. I'm Free. Jesus is here. You spoke to me. God you got my back. No weapon.

I said, no weapon formed against me shall prosper without your permission. Halleluiah right now."

Even those that walked by his house heard him praising God and slowed down a bit to look at his door and window to listen as if they expected someone to come out. His neighbors, who stood out front talking, stopped talking to listen and to see why he was praising God so loudly, and to hear what he was saying. Some said that he must have been going crazy. Another said that he must be one of those Jesus freaks. Other said that they

The Perfect Lesson

felt sorry for his wife. And a few said that maybe he is a Christian. But a prominent member of the hood said, "No- way: Christians don't act like that, unless they are at church. That's when they start jumping-up and down having a fit, and scrambling on the floor, but not when they are at home." He went on to say, "Shucks sir, if he keeps this up he'll soon be doing that out here in the streets man. You see, that's a sign of the times man. Now people are doing all kinds of shit and call theirself a Christian. Like my moms used to say, 'You got to do more then just be 'hoop'n' and holl'n'. Jesus might come back right now and say I aint never known you buddy'. You feel me man?"

But inside the house, Zeek was elated as he sat there and enjoyed every morsel of his cold meal. As he sat there a growing hunger for the 'word' began to develop within him. The TV was on in front of him, but his mind was on tomorrow and the holy gospel and on ministry work but the way his eyes was aiming, it look like he was glued to the tube.

Gathering The Sheep

At home Giz was busy searching thru his files and gathering the flock with more zeal and enthusiasm then he ever found inside of himself at any point in his life. He even posted a reminder on his refrigerator to himself to call Jerry. Jerry was

Young Darby

an old friend of Giz who was always in and out of trouble with the law. Most of his jail time was on account of stealing cars, and drug dealings.

He was released on parole a few years ago.

The last stretch was 22 years, for a murder beef. Eventhough, the specific murder weapon was never found, he was convicted basically due to a lack of legal research by his own lawyers, Gopher and Wallace, bad timing, and a familiar judge: for this particular judge once told him prior to his murder conviction, that if he ever came back before her again for anything, not even a Lock Smith of Lock Smiths would be able to unlock the lock.

Nevertheless until this day, he still maintains his innocence. Jerry, Giz, and Zeek practically grew-up together. And mostly everyone that knows him, believe that he did not do it. Unfortunately, Jerry was still experimenting with crack and weed. He was very frail and wore his hair kind of nappy, wrapped with a 'doo rag', and wore his jeans barely hanging below his buttocks as was supposed to have been the style. Today when Giz saw his reminder on the refrigerator to call Jerry, he phoned him.

"Yo! Wa'd-up Dog?" Jerry answered.

"Hey Brother Jerry it's me, just trying to make sure you don't forget tomorrow is Sunday and that your 'boy' is gonna be ready for you. He also requested that you have a front row seat so he can

The Perfect Lesson

shine the light on you, because you never was rapped to tight, he told me."

"What? That sorry-ass mother...Excuse me man! That wanna-be-preacher! Man let me get my hands on him. I don't care preacher or not. I dare him say that in my face. Um gonna be right on the front mother shoven row."

Giz was excited, "Well brother Jerry I aint saying no more. But I will say this last thing. At first I had some doubts about him trying to hit on your sister, cause I know when he first joined the church he used to say he always keep her in his special prayers with special request. I never really knew what that meant, nor questioned it, but he also have been saying this about a few of the other sisters here———-Man, can you keep a secret?"

"Yeah man, I don't jive know anybody at yo church that I jive talk to Dog. Who um gonna tell? You know what I'm sayin'?"

"Man, he told me that he want to screw 'em."

"What? Screw who?"

"The very chicks, I mean the very young up-right respectable sisters at the church that he suppose to be doing them special request prayers for."

"Now you see why I don't be goin' to church man? Aint nothin' but hypocrites up in that joint Joe! And he's the main one."

"Man, I'm telling ya'."

Young Darby

"Dog, y'all got a devil in y'all church Joe!"

"Man it's bad. I know."

"Dog, you probably the only one up in there 'bout somethin' Joe. That's why me and you still down 'dog'!' I know it's been a long time since I stepped foot into anybody church, but if the good Lord give me strength and wake me up one more 'gin, um comin' to your church tomorrow Joe. Un'stand what 'um sayin' Dog?"

"Cool baby! But when you come man, can you do me one favor?

"Sure Dog! Wud -up?"

Don't be calling me 'Dog', man. And Bring Ann with you, she need to have her eyes open too. Can you do that?"

"Sure you right 'dog' um gonna try to bring her too, she need to see this bastard. She don't do anything on Sunday anyway but wash her car and stare at herself in the mirror. Ya'll gonna have any food up in that joint Dog, I mean dude, I mean Deacon?"

"Yes–sir, if you come early. The missionaries makes a light breakfast with bacon, eggs, grits, biscuits, coffee cake, coffee and juices every third Sunday, and a kicking lunch with the works after morning service. Just tell Ann wipe the snot off the little rug-rats faces before she bring'em. I don't want any snot in my food or hanging from the table. Understand?"

The Perfect Lesson

Jerry laughed, saying, "Awe Deacon, get out of here Dog. How much the chow gonna set me back?"

"It's free. We don't charge not one dime."

"For real?"

"For real! Tell you what, if anybody tries to charge you for somethin', let me know. Just let me know. I'll take care of it.

"Man, you on! Thanks deacon man. You alright! See you tomorrow!"

"Ok Good Brother!"

Deacon Giz made more calls enticing more to come, as he did Jerry, using food and negative aspects about Zeek's past to get them to come, and many took the bate.

Now Giz felt great accomplishment as he sat back and looked up to the Lord saying,

"Lord, you know we got to get them into your house the best way we can, and your word say that we should be as wise as serpents but as harmless as doves. I just thank you Jesus for helping me to be wise. Lord, please continue to help me that I might be even wiser. I might know a lot, but I think there is still probably more for me to know. In Jesus name. Amen."

Can You Feel it?

It was Sunday Morning. Deacon Zeek peeled his covers back as Sunday morning unfolded her factory wrapped packaged beauty. As the morning's sweet savory fragrances seeped and whispered in thru his curtains surrounding him in his room, his legs emerged from his covers and his toes reached for the floor.

The melodious echoing tunes of the gentle breezes enchanted his mode and the radiant sunrays beamed thru the window perfecting a dominant spotlight circle upon his floor. At this moment, both feet touched down in the center of this brilliant circle.

Thru the cracked windows, the cool breeze began to softly part his laced curtains, revealing the huge trees and leaf's colors of oranges, reds, yellows and browns as if they were waiting for orders to sway, bend, bow or move. A Large flock of birds cruised over and set upon and around his fence and gateposts as if also waiting for the command to fly loops, chirp or sing, as they seem to have been looking in Zeek's window. The odd shaped clouds with fluffy carved eyes, stood still as waiting for orders to morph into new forms. The sky was calmly commanding, 'peace to be still'.

The Perfect Lesson

Zeek knelled down on both knees and prayed to the God of his salvation. When he finished praying he even felt like, he, himself, was also waiting for something to happen or maybe that he had forgotten something.

He woke-up Ellen and went to the bathroom. Ellen stood in her room also momentarily spellbound by today's magnificent array of serene scenery.

Their rose garden was in full bloom, packed with colorful azaleas blossoming in an array of assorted smiling formed deciduous leaves. She too, lingered there observing the various species of birds.

There was even a crow among robins and blue jays and what looked like a buzzard setting alone on the left corner fence post.

They all were just sitting there on her fence quietly as if waiting for something to take place.

She seemed puzzled, nevertheless, kneeled and prayed as well.

After they both freshen-up and dressed, they took each other's hands and prayed again, but this time for strength and an unselfish and uncompromising 'free-course word', and for holy direction, in Jesus' name, then got everything ready and departed to church. Most of the time Ellen normally would be talking, but today, Zeek noticed his wife was calm and quiet as if she was waiting for him to initiate

Young Darby

any conversation today. Today it was obvious that Ellen had decided to surrender her 'all' to Zeek's complete will. She was content. Conversely, Zeek felt an overwhelming strong desire to say something, but not much. Ellen remained comfortably quiet thru out the ride to church. Zeek began to feel like his seat was burning red-hot so he began to speed up a bit. Eventhough Ellen observed that he was more then a little over the speed limit she smiled to herself this time, but still said nothing. Once they reached the church and parked, he slowly leaned towards Ellen, gently kissing her on her lips, and reminded her to stay in prayer. She squeezed and petted his hands, looked into his eyes, one last time, with 'I Love you' smeared on her face, then Zeek dashed off.

On his way to his office, he knocked on the pastor's already halfway opened door.

The pastor lifted his head without smiling and said, "Are you ready?"

The deacon responded, "Yes sir…..um… … Which service?"

The Pastor stared at him for a moment and only his mouth moved as he said, "This one."

Zeek momentarily closed his eyes, opened them, inhaled deeply gathering much wind in his mouth until his jaws was well full and rounded, then slowly blew it out, exhaling as an athlete who have just finished working out, then nodded an affirming head to the pastor, softly saying, "Thank you!" and went to his office.

Let The Service Begin

In the meanwhile the people were pouring in from all available entrances. The seats were quickly filling up. Jerry, Ann, Moe, Larry, Mike and a host of other long past associates of Zeek and Giz, who were invited by Giz, was seated very close up front excited and engaged in conversation. It looked like they were having a private reunion. The church soon became packed beyond capacity again, with some folks standing and leaning on the walls. More chairs were scrounged-up and brought in and still some folks were leaning along the walls. And the Choir began to sing. Deacon Giz strolled around with both hands resting on his belt with both thumbs tugging and plucking on his suspender-bands while sporting a very hearty smile as he went greeting various members, but giving special greetings and encouraging words to the twenty or more guests that he had invited and persuaded to come today. He was so happy you could see nothing but his yellowing teeth as he smiled and whispered to his fellow brotherhood of deacons.

Casually he informed them that he had invited these lost souls to an opportunity of repentance and salvation before it was too late. He specifically pointing out that Jerry was an ex con, who use to be locked-up for murder. His fellow deacons marveled at how many souls that Giz persuaded to come.

Before long the word quickly spread, that Deacon Giz was Zeek's main man and a true on fire disciple of God regardless of that misunderstanding they had in the hall the other-day and that this was clear proof of Deacon's Giz faith.

Giz proudly went over to several of his invitees reminding them to share by whom they were invited, when the welcome committee asks' them to stand, and how they heard about this church. He informed his invitees, that in doing so, everyone would recognize them after service when they go into the fellowship hall to have the special lunch that was being prepared.

When the welcome announcement was made, over thirty visitors stood-up, and most of them were invited by Deacon Giz and they also announced that Deacon Giz was the reason why they were encouraged to come and fellowship today. Deacon Giz received much praise, attention, and salutations from many, and the clergy in the pulpit approvingly

The Perfect Lesson

nodded their heads saying, "Praise God." And "My, my, my," as they looked over, acknowledging Deacon Giz and motioned with their hands for him to stand-up. And he graciously stood-up making a modest bow, but with the palms of his hands, signaling everyone, with a modest expression on his smiling face that it was nothing.

After seeing all of these new souls today, some even started a rumor that Deacon Giz was a 'real on fire for God' street minister and Man of God that was always walking in the Holy Ghost. Some said he was God's most valuable Deacon at Zion.

After all of the applause ceased, the announcer said, "The next voice that you will hear after the selection will be none other then our very own man of God, The Honorable Deacon Zeek with The Holy Word, that we all have been waiting for. Deacon Giz frowned on hearing such an introduction as he looked over at Jerry, subtly motioning with his head and forming the words with his mouth, 'holy my ass'.

Jerry looked back at Giz and shook his head and they both smiled and snickered like only they knew the secret joke. Deacon Giz looked at certain others whom he invited with this look and gesture and they too seemed to have understood the secret behind Giz secret mischievous smile and his subtle motioning of the lips. Nevertheless Giz carried on clapping his hands and shuffling his shoulders like this was the greatest day in his life.

Deacon Zeek was now kneeling down in front of his chair in the pulpit praying, and his chair seemed to have been on fire or was too hot to sit in. When he fanned his backside in his office before he came out, it stopped momentarily, but when he started walking towards the sanctuary, and the closer he came to the pulpit, the more his backside burned. He could not set in his office seat or in the pulpit chair nor did he understand why this burning sensation has occurred and would not cease.

But like a ready primed fighter, he could not wait for the bell to ring or for the chorus to stop singing.

Since he could not sat down he did not want to rush the choir by standing, so he continued to remain kneeling in front of his chair in the pulpit, eventhough his knees was beginning to weaken from the pain from kneeling on the pulpit's hardwood floor.

To the audience he looked like he was praying, but he was now agonizing over his throbbing knee pain and burning buttocks.

When he noticed the chorus winding down, he slowly stood-up while slowly exhaling, and saying to himself, "Thank you Jesus."

The Perfect Lesson

He drew to the podium like a 'prize fighter' entering into the ring. All was silent. Even the gum chewers stopped chewing. It was so silent you could hear asthmatics slightly wheezing, hay fever sufferers breathing, and rushing winds winding along the stained windows.

Giz looked around and marveled at the silence. Pastor Gateway was moved and impressed by this great presents of silence with heart pounding anticipation among such a great mass. And Deacon Zeek was poised as he looked out over the congregation.

Zeek first thanked the pastor for this opportunity to speak again. He thanked all visitors for coming and the official church body and all members for coming and attending this great gathering. The colorful attire worn throughout the audience of the congregation suddenly reminded Zeek of his rose garden and the birds he saw surrounding his yard this morning.

Giz reminded him of the buzzard. Zeek looked up into the ceiling and a few birds were there looking down thru the circular glass window at him, standing still but flapping it's wings in mid air.

And he began: "I'm going to be direct and brief so please bare with me because at the sametime I want to take my time. You see, the last time I spoke about the many blessings of God and the great generosities of God, the goodness, kindness, patience, love and long suffering of God the Father and his salvation. Today I want to complete that message."

Deacon Giz smiled and shouted, "Take your time. Take your time. Make it clear."

Deacon Zeek continued: "There is one thing that trouble man on the face of the earth to his ruin. Now please understand, like the bible, when I use the word man I'm also referring to woman, thus mankind. For, we are all mankind. I believe the Bible did it like this because woman came from man.

Without man there would be no woman and afterwards, without woman there could not be another man, unless God made another man without using a woman as he did in the beginning according to his word, Amen?

I will be thankful to the Lord if I can at least complete part of my point. Just by a show of hands, raise your hand if you believe you are on your way to heaven, Zion and visitors?"

It looked like nearly everyone raised his or her hand.

He continued: "The Title of my message today is, '**The Logic Of Lust And The Hidden Message**'. When I'm done, you will understand the logic of lust, and I hope with my whole heart that you would have also uncovered the hidden message.

The Perfect Lesson

As a premise please turn to Phil. 3:14-15, where Paul said, 'I press toward the mark for the prize of the high calling of God in Jesus Christ.' And 'Let us therefore, as many as be perfect, be thus minded: and if in anything ye be otherwise minded, God shall reveal even this unto you.'

I got news for you church, if you are still lying and cursing you aint going nowhere, because it's evident you're not pressing towards the mark. All of us in here today that say we love Jesus, aught to be 'thus minded'.

What is Paul referring to here when he said we aught to be 'thus minded'? He is referring to, 'as many as be perfect'. Also, if you are committing fornication or adultery and die in that state without repenting, you are not pressing toward the mark. The bible makes it clear that no whoremonger, no deceiver, thief, fornicator, adulterer or murderer will enter into the Kingdom."

Giz began to clear his throat and Shirley and Jerry looked over and acknowledged Giz's mischievous smile.

The Logic Of Lust

Now for my Point! My brother and sisters, our biggest enemy is our own flesh.

Young Darby

Because our flesh wants what it wants regardless of the consequences. To our flesh getting what it want is the only thing that's logical.

The logic of the flesh is to always feel good at any cost. In other words, whatever the flesh can make you do to receive a pleasurable sensation, that's what it's gonna try to make you do, even if it cost you all of your money, your family, your wife, husband or even if it cost you your life.

That's why when you feel the lust level rising in your body and the craving of the flesh to receive, it's just that, and that only.

Lust is void of understanding, absent of wisdom and alienated from love. Because of the imposing influence of lust is so hard to ignore, it doesn't mean that you no longer love your husband or your wife, life or God. When you feel lust surfacing, remember, it must at times, because lust, fornication, and adulterous offences must come.

It is when one goes to the extent of allowing these lustful cravings to be satisfied, is when we miss the mark, and all hell breaks lose.

And surely, when these lustful feelings arise, and one fantasizes committing immoral act, it does not necessarily mean that one does not love their husband or wife. It means, you have been temporarily weaken and set-up by lust. So, it is when one succumbs to the antics of the logic of lust, that they become weaken and taken by there

The Perfect Lesson

own lust and thus, placing their soul in jeopardy of hell fire.

This also shows a lack of wisdom, control, maturity and intelligence to chose the correct response or answer to what I would like to call, The Flesh-logical Examination of life. Because of lust's relentless persistence in dominating our will, some may never pass this quiz, termed, The Flesh-logical Examination, therefore would not qualify to take the Final: so their exam paper would be, unfortunately collected possibly prematurely.

During this quiz, when the wrong response is selected, it is critical for that person to repent and never go that way again, or chose that response again, which is the second opportunity to the second part of this quiz to press for the prize of the high calling in God in Christ Jesus. Thus, therefore, each quiz or test question has two parts, and two potential chances to make it right.

But please be reminded, that it is still possible to lose you life sooner or later by giving a wrong or ungodly answer or response with your life, because we respond to the tests of life with our lifestyle. Word entries do not count alone. When one finally gives in to this lustful craving of the body to the point of satisfying it, the power of the lust craving immediately becomes weak.

During this period, lust has minimal power and influence, and the power of ones own mind and ones spirit can then emerge and dominate the will.

The Window

During this window of time, one could actually face-up to, and see clean clear thru their faults for what they are and may feel regret if they have at least an ounce of God's consciousness in them equivalent to the size of a mustered seed. Then they may say, '…why did I do that?' Or 'I wish I did not do that.' And, 'I'm not gonna do it again.' You can say this then because you have already sinned: satisfied the lust craving and while it's power is down, the spirit man power is up, because during this window of time, the flesh has no present foe, adversary, no opponent, no competitor, or tester to test it strength, because during this down time, lust and wanting is satisfied.

This period of time is a critical window in which self-discovery can also be realized, dealt with, and understood. This doesn't only applies to the lust involving sex, but also applies to the lust for the use of drugs, alcohol and cigarettes, and to all that involves pleasing the flesh, including lying,

The Perfect Lesson

cheating, murder, gossiping, manipulating, and any acts against humanity.

So if you ever commit any type of sin again, remember the window. This window can also be used to escape if used wisely and with the understanding of it's function. If used unwisely can lead to deep depression. Once you use the things or done the thing(s) that temporarily satisfies the flesh cravings, it's power is down for a short period of time. During this window or flesh-craving down-time, the flesh is busy digesting the filth of it's desires and therefore it's attention, desires, motivations and energy is exclusively diverted to digesting the filth only during this critical period, and the 'spirit man' power can now operate unhindered. That's why one can smoke and or drink alcohol and shortly afterwards, during this window, can say that they can stop anytime they want with evident confidence, but hours later, they are right back in the craving."

The congregation was quiet but ever so attentive, Zeek paused and rest his hands upon his waist as if resting his case.

Chapter 10
The Lust Foe

"Now he who has an ear, let him hear, what I'm about to teach you about this foe.

Lust communicates to us all, via projecting 'pseudo illusional preexperiential situational conditions', allowing pseudo projections suggestions of illusioned sensations and perceptions of a pseudo state, thus overwhelming one's present will and usual state of mind, making it inevitable for someone to commit the act. But woe, to the simpletons that does.

In essence, the chemistry of lust produces a preponderance of sensual stimulating waves of surreal pleasure, associated with and linked to prior similar and same pleasurable experiences. The presence of which seeks to instinctively alter our normal conscious mind-set, aided pheromonally, which is the use of sensual and sexual scents biologically produced by the opposite sex and by our desire to engage in sexual activity.

Hence, the presence and strength of lust, though psychologically and chemically based, was given unto us as a test, because as you can see, the correct answer to this test involves and consist of responsible godly attributes, mature reasoning, self

The Perfect Lesson

control, integrity, nobility, humility, long suffering, sacrifice, righteousness, understanding, character and evidence that one communicate often or regularly with the holy spirit, whom I also call, 'The Keeper'.

This means that your answer to the logic of lust is not just a simple word or just saying 'no', but a conscious and dedicated purposeful 'no' that consciously and deliberately consist of all of the ingredients above, enforced by your lifestyle and conversation."

At this point you could hear the congregation exhaling as if on their second wind.

"Are you still with me?" he asked the congregation.

Various individuals shouted, "Teach the truth!"

Some simply said, "Lord have mercy!"

And many shook their heads as if, now they knew why they were having such a hard time wrestling with their flesh, but some still looked lost with question marks tattooed on their foreheads, saying that the speaker was too deep, that they had to get the tape.

For the first time, the pastor noticed that many of the regular members were actually taking notes, and there was no whispering. No one was sleeping, even Deacon Giz curiously eyeballed the congregation for looks of oppositions, but could not find one, nor could he get the attention of any

Young Darby

of his invitees anymore, for their eyes were now glued front and centered.

Deacon Zeek went on: "Don't misunderstand me, lust is a real foe, which also qualifies it as a real test of who we are, how godly or ungodly we are and how strong we are. Yes! And how weak we are. So don't think its strange when you experience this, for you are still living in your body, so you can not be exempt, even if you are an ordain minister of the gospel praying night and day.

The Bible tells us that we have not been experiencing anything that Jesus has not. That's right, Jesus was also confronted with the same test. There is no temptation that confronts us that did not confront Jesus. Which means he was presented with every opportunity to sin as well as being tempted at every point. Do you believe that Jesus was going to be the only one tempted, and tested and not you and I? My fellow brothers and sisters, we must be tempted, tested and tried. This is the only way that we can prove ourselves to be the true children of God and to show that we are somethin' like him, if not just like him.

The Lesson

We are on the testing grounds. Planet earth is our testing ground and the Lord is molding, making

The Perfect Lesson

and remaking us, day by day, unto a perfect way, unto a perfect day, and unto a perfect God.

Just like when you went to school, you couldn't go on to the next level until you met certain conditions, past certain test by selecting the appropriate answers to prove that you knew what the test giver was challenging you on.

God has the same right and responsibility to administer such a test, but is the original tester as well as the Master tester and the designer of his own test.

However, the test that he gives cannot be completed with paper and ink. Instead of us using paper and ink, he requires us to use the ink of our living intentions, the living issues of our heart, our way of life, and our conversations, written on the paper of time.

He knew we would at first mess-up, so for scratch-paper, he has given us our preadolescent years. Just in case we continued to mess-up, he has given us the eraser of forgiveness. So if you mess-up, it's important that you use the eraser right away.

Now just like our earthly tests and teachers has certain time requirements imposed, our Father God has also given us a time-frame in which we must complete the test, and if we drag along and don't complete it in the allotted time authorized, he will send one of his assistants over to pulled the paper of time when the examination period is over and sometimes sooner. So that is why it is good for us to erase, and correct all mistakes as soon as we discover them so we may maximize our time, and he is well able to give us more paper if we show good cause. And certainly, just as our earthly appointed teachers notifies us with a two minute warning that our test time is almost up, so do our Heavenly Fathers notify us with subtle knowledge, and sometimes visions and sometimes dreams, or sometimes it could be with a word, that our time is about up. But if we approach each test reasonably well, we know we atleast have the minimal time he quoted us in his word or in the master's manual, if you will, to complete the test. At the end of the day, or when all is said and done, we are graded on the responses that we gave to the test. Remember, once the exam time is up, it's all over. So we must use the 'paper of time' wisely. That's why by design, our first teachers were programmed to teach us by love instinctively, cause it was so vital that we understood in our 'scratch paper period', right from wrong and the basic instructions in wisdom in order to be successful at the next level.

Because at the next level, in the pure 'paper of time phase', all instruction would be basically given most of the time, absent of love, and the personal and dynamic ingredients required for essential passionate conviction, growth, and development to

The Perfect Lesson

live a godly life. But we received these instructions and essential ingredients in our early years, our 'pre-scratch paper' years and during our 'scratch paper years'.

Paper Of Time

Thus, during the 'paper of time' period, providing we absorbed properly from our first teachers, during our 'scratch paper period', we would have the analytical abilities to differentiate between meaningful loving instructions and academia, and hence, allowing us to eat all instructions in life as fish, but tossing away the bones of imperfections.

Thankfully, the Father has also made available, and has given us progress reports every Sunday, by means of one of his most trained ministers. Some of us consider this report each Sunday from his ministers; some don't. Just like in the worldly school system where report cards and progress reports are given regularly, so does God give reports regularly.

Father God gives these reports so we can know where we are along the way. Some don't care, they just want to go home and play, but some do care. The Lord have built-in many helps along our path and journey in order to insure our perfection and the development of our faith so that we would have to work extremely hard in not acknowledging him, not to pass the test. Like most people really want to finish school and hear the teacher say to them, 'Well done', and see their name placed on the Honor Roll and even win a prize or an award when all is said and done, so would we all like for Jesus to say to us on that last day, 'Well done', and see our names written in the Book Of Life, and receive a Crown Of Life. How do I know these things to be true? I'm glad you asked!"

Deacon Zeek paused, resting his hand on his waist, and looked at Jerry and Ann sating there in the middle third row with their mouths wide open and said, "Jerry is sating right there, he can tell you how I was probably the biggest hypocrites he had ever known. Some years ago, I even lied to him just to lay up with his sister, while I knew he must have known that I had already proposed to one of his sister's friends. You see, then, it didn't bother me much because at the time, I was not saved, and I knew I wasn't tryin' to do right.

During that period in my life, I greatly underestimated the ability, conviction, determination and tools of lust. I did not understand accurately the difference between lust and love. I just wanted to hit and run, y'all know what I mean! Now y'all looking at me like y'all surprise or somethin'."

Chuckles of understanding echoed throughout the congregation.

"I haven't always been saved folks. I don't know about you, but I use to smoke a pack of Kools

The Perfect Lesson

a day with my 'Colt 45', and be looking for butts outside on the ground early the next morning. Then he shouted: Where you out there?"

Private chuckles continued throughout the congregation.

Zeek continued, "But thank God, he done delivered me from that. Yeah, I flunked quite a few of the master's test and quizzes, but thank God for periodic intermittent teachers of the gospel and regular progress reports to put the light on where I was missing it. And Hallelujah! Thank him for the eraser of forgiveness. I'm still requesting the eraser now and then. You see, I thought I was going to die with a 'smoke' in my hand, or alcohol or a narcotic habit but his grace was sufficient and his power was almighty."

Shouts and praises rumbled and roared throughout the congregation.

"At one point I smoked so much weed, that I even tried to grow it in my backyard so I could smoke it and sell it myself whenever I wanted to, cause I got tired of running around the corner tryin' to find somebody to give my money to. But I had one problem. It wouldn't grow. Everytime I saw a few leaves on it, I had to smoke 'em. I never could give it time to grow. I smoked it faster than it could grow a leaf. Even the stems became my delight. But I have to thank God again, because he delivered me from that. I hope y'all don't mine me telling on myself for a minute."

Now the congregation was buzzing with private quips and private testimonies and whispering to one another, confessing what they have done as well as what God had also delivered them from.

Deacon Zeek continued: "Not to long ago, in the very recent past, I wanted every women my eyes could see, didn't care how they looked as long as they had a fat butt. Ask Deacon Giz! Oh yes! The good Deacon, he'll tell ya'. And guess what? God delivered me from that. You see my brothers and sisters; I am an authority on the subject of sin, lust, flesh and forgiveness. I didn't learn about sin, lust and forgiveness just by reading about it. I was lust number one victim and toy. Like Paul said, we aught not be ignorant of the devil devices. I'm not proud about it, but I believe that I was at one time one of the biggest sinners in this church, and probably of this whole State.

Moreover, I believe that no one in this church have out sinned me, and probably, never will, eventhough I have already repented and am done with sin. Cause now, I believe the only way I can sin is by accident or thru ignorance.

And that should be the only way any child of God should be able to sin. We should not be caught in our right mind sinning with full knowledge that we are sinning before a just and holy God and

The Perfect Lesson

calling ourself a Christian. Now what kind of man was I Deacon Giz?"

Deacon Giz rocked forward like he was about to stand and started scratching his head, with a shallow voice, shaking his head, saying, "I hear you now Deacon."

"You see Deacon Giz, I found out that the purpose of the female butt had the same function of the male butt. Did you know that?"

Laughter rolled throughout the audience, and Giz sat there with tight lips, nodding his head as if in serious agreement.

"You see Deacon Giz, The female Butt, though shapely, and sexy, and may or may not be attached to a pretty face, is also not the cleanest part of the body nor could you truly keep it clean, because by nature it was made to get rid of waste and to be a foul area. But on my way here today, I was looking around and I still saw people looking at each other butts. For what?"

The congregation seemed to have been on a slight role with the grins and, "He,he,hes," and "Haw, haw, haws."

Zeek continued: "The only thing decent, right or good that you can do with somebody else's ass, is to wipe it. Amen?"

Many members now being shocked into laughter, laughed out-loud, many shook their head, and whispering was heard throughout the place.

Young Darby

Chuckles and giggling roared even from the missionary and deacons' section: even Deacon Giz tight-set lips reluctantly loosen into a piece of a mean smile.

Gateway tried feverishly to maintain his composure by hiding his face and bowing his head to muffle his laughs. Delores was blushing with a hand to her mouth. Kenney and Mark were constantly encouraging and urging Zeek to preach.

And Zeek continued, "My brothers and sister, God is raising up a standard. God said no abuser of themselves, fornicator, adulterer, nor deceiver shall make it into the Kingdom.

What good is it to have all of the finest things that life have to offer you right now, then die and, and on top of that, burn in a lake of fire forever and ever?

My brothers and sisters, God said, 'Be perfect'. And he put everything in place in order for you to get a perfect grade and have your name placed on the Honor Role when the exam is over."

Does God Really Want Me Perfect Right Now?

Zeek stood still for a moment and said, "Why y'all looking at me like that? You heard me right. When you know all your stuff at school, and your teacher give you a perfect grade of 'A' in class

The Perfect Lesson

for your coursework, and you end-up with your name on the Honor Role because of your perfect attendance and work, you don't have no problem with that, do you?

That's right! You worked hard! You have to be a perfect student or close to it, or do perfect or near perfect work in order to get a perfect or near perfect grade. Do you know that when your academic teacher tells you that they know that you can make all 'A's, they are actually saying, 'If you want, you could be a perfect student'.

When your employer or company tells you that you could be their C.E.O. or Top Producer, what they are really saying is that, you could be the perfect employee or leader.

When your parents told you that you could become whoever you decide to become and that the sky was the limit and that you can achieve whatever you can dream, they were telling you that you could be perfect, and that they don't care what anyone else say, there aint nothing wrong with you.

No wonder, those that are missing upper and lowers limbs are driving better then many with all of their limbs.

And when Jesus said, 'Be ye therefore perfect, even as your Father which is in heaven is perfect', he was saying that you can be perfect, and he don't care what anybody else say, and we should believe he meant what he said, and said what he meant.

Sometimes it looks like we are ready to believe everybody else except Jesus.

Now remember, he did not say try to be perfect. He said be perfect. He did not say if you try to be perfect, he would help you. He said be ye perfect even as the father in heaven is also perfect. He qualified how he wants us to be perfect, by saying, 'as our Father'. In other words, he defined perfection for us so we could not say that we didn't know how he wanted us to be perfect, or ask, what did he mean by being perfect, or that the dictionary was unclear. Church, are you aware that Jesus said that he is coming back for a people without spot or blemish. Not for people with spots and blemishes. After saying that, do you believe that he's comin' back for people with spots and blemishes? If you do, you either have a gigantic size problem in understanding what he's sayin', or with the language or perhaps a denial problem.

I believe he's coming back for people he loves, like, A'sa for instance. For, in 1Kings, 15:14 it says, '…A'-sa's heart was perfect with the Lords all of his days.'

Now that's a huge testimony. This guy pleased God, and kept his word his entire life. Evidently, God is not a respecter of persons, and he believes that since A'sa kept his word and walked before him perfectly all of his days, you and I can do the samething."

The Perfect Lesson

"For The Upright Shall Dwell In The Land And The Perfect Shall Remain In It."

Prov.2:21

"That's a heavy testimony aint it? It's not about how God bless him so much, but about how he blessed the Lord with a perfect heart so much that God honored him in his holy word to be an example and as proof that it can be done, and that we can be perfect before God if we chose. Some of us believe you can have a perfect heart and don't have perfect behavior before God. I got news for you my friend.

You can also have perfect behavior, because a perfect heart produces perfect work. For, a perfect heart equals perfect behavior, because psalm 101:2 says, 'I will behave myself wisely in a perfect way. O when wilt thou come unto me? I will walk within my house with a perfect heart.' You see if you have a perfect heart, then you can behave yourself in a perfect way, and the Lord knows this. That's why he tells us to be perfect. He wants to bless us in a perfect way.

And A'-sa was not the only one. Did you know that? There was a man in the land of Uz, whose name was Job; and that man was perfect and upright, and one that feared God and eschewed evil,' according to Job 1:1. He was perfect and upright.

My friends, I submit to you today that the Lord wants us to be perfect and upright before him, because God bragged on Job, in Job 1:8, when he asked Satan, '....Hast thou considered my servant Job, that there is none like him in the earth, a perfect and an upright man, one that feareth God and escheweth evil?'

Haaalliluuuuja! I'm convinced today that the Lord wants us upright and perfect regardless if you believe it or not.

And it was the psalmist who said in, 18:32, 'It is God that girdeth me with strength, and maketh my way perfect.'

So people, if we determined to be perfect, he will make our way perfect as well. Do you want peace now and forever? Then heed the psalmist who went even further to say in, 37:37, 'Mark the perfect man, and behold the upright: for the end of that man is peace'. The Lord said that you could mark the perfect man and keep the one who walk upright in your mind because in the end he will be the one in peace and you will know it. Now I must admit, I'm not a rocket scientist, but if I were to follow the logic in this scripture it would follow that if a man is walking in imperfection the end of that man would be in ruin.

My friend, I submit to you that it is our job to be perfect and to make our calling sure? I submit to you, that you are saved as long as you stay saved. Not as long as you try to be saved. So it's up to us to make our salvation sure, it's not automatic. For the

The Perfect Lesson

word said that those that endure until the end shall be saved. Not those that start the race or is baptized are guaranteed to win, but those that finish the race. The Bible said that we should make our salvation sure. So then, just because you came to church and was baptized, it don't mean that you are guaranteed a spot in heaven. Got news for you buddy, you can come here every Sunday and still go straight to hell.

I don't care how much you pray and how many times you say, 'Hallelujah', you still can go to hell. I don't care how many times you come to church and have what some may call a holy ghost fit and dance a jig, if your heart is not right before God and you are not walking upright before him with a perfect heart you still can go to hell."

Deacon Zeek paused, and began motioning with his hands for all to join in as he continued saying, "You can sing on the choir. You can be the head deacon, the best dressed usher, and faithfully give tithes and offering, become a vegetarian, feed the hungry, but if your heart is not perfect before God, *you still can...*"

And in unison, the congregation harmoniously shouted, "Go to hell."

Deacon Zeek continued, "You must continue in the words and the ways of the Lord and pay attention to those progress report. Or else you just might open up the door one day and find yourself in hell my brother and sister with burning flames

Young Darby

wrapped around your ungodly ass and no one would be able to shut the door. Yes in deed! God do want you to have everything you desire, but he also wants you to give him everything he desires. Giving is a two way street.

We always want God to give us everything and don't want to give nothing to God but a prayer and a shout and two dollars. We got to give God everything and stop perpetrating a fraud. We must stop acting like we don't understand what he already has done for us and what he wants from us.

We're down here talkin' bout, we wish we knew what God wanted us to do. Only if he would tell me, I would do it, we say.'"

With burning eyes of passion, Zeek continued, "Well my friends, God is speaking to you right now. He's saying: 'Be perfect. Walk upright. Do good to all men. Love your neighbor as you love yourself. Pray for your leaders. Feed the hungry. Visit the sick and the shut in. Pray without ceasing. Love the Lord with all your heart, soul mind and might. Spread the gospel. Be strong. Go thru your trials and tribulations like a good soldier. Prosper. Walk by faith. Walk as Jesus walked. Stop sinning. Turn the other Cheek. Endure hardship like a good soldier. Worship the almighty God and endure until the end'. Study to show yourself approved. He's saying, seek me.

The Perfect Lesson

Bless the fatherless, elderly, widows and the poor.'

You see, he already have given us everything when he gave his only son, and we still want him to give us more. Some of us have made him a Genie, asking him to zap up a car, houses and plenty of money. And the sad part about it is, we don't even want to walk perfect and upright before him even if he did it. Some of us don't even want to believe that God want us to walk before him perfectly, so how can we believe that we can? We got to believe what he's saying first.

Don't misunderstand me, I believe that God don't have any problem in blessing us above and beyond our imagination, but what we fail to understand is, he already done it. He already done it. He already done it. Say it till it sinks in. This part here, is the meat, and is for adults only. Adults in the word, that is! He already done it!

He's An Already Done It God

What kind of God do we serve? He already gave us his only begotten son, so what more do we want? Jesus done came down here and suffered more than any man.

He was humiliated, tormented, suffered, condemned to death, beaten, mistreated, treated like a slave, mocked, spat on, lied on, tied-up, talked about, laughed at, stripped of his garment in public, stripped of his dignity before many, made poor, scoffed at, whipped, crucified, cheated, made mired, disfigured, nailed to a tree and left for dead, then hung until dead. He died hanging nailed to a tree for you and for me and with his last dying breath he prayed to God the Father 'to forgive us, man that is, for they (we) know not what they (we) do'.

But he didn't stop there he went on down to hell on the devil's turf and whopped Satin's unholy ass in his own house. Took the keys of death from him, looked death in the eyes, stripped death of his sting, and with the same power he use to lay his life down, he used it to take it back up again and left his grave empty, then stood-up, fold-up his garments, laid them in his borrowed tomb, walked out from the tomb's cave and said, 'Oh death! Where is your sting? Oh grave, where is your victory?'

The congregation began praising God with clapping, shouting and dancing. Over the thunderous praises of the congregation, Deacon Zeek voice climbed even higher as he continued preaching.

"As a mighty warrior; The living Lord of Lords; The Prince of Peace; The All Mighty King of King; The First and The Last; The Rose; The Bright Morning Star; The Lily of the Valley. He who died, but behold he lives, and with the marks

The Perfect Lesson

still in his hands, he stood there victorious with the devil made his foot-stool, and with death's stinger hanging from his powerful hand. Everybody aught' a shout Hallelujah."

The congregation was already on their feet praising God.

"So then, as it says in 1Kings 8:61, 'Let your heart therefore be perfect with the Lord our God, to walk in his statues, and to keep his commandments, as at this day.'"

And the sanctuary was filled with the awesome presents of the Lord so much so that there was a great smell of bountiful flowers, roses, and lilies.

The fragrances of rosebuds flooded everyone nostrils but no one could comprehend it. Maybe you can smell them now.

Zeek tried a few times to regain control, but the people was intensely caught up in praise and worship, shouting, some speaking in tongues, some got out from there wheelchairs, and many laid stretched out on the floor crying. Some ran along the isles as if on fire and the glory of the Lord was apparent. Zeek bowed and shook his head as he stood there swaying back and forth as he watched and was in awe of what the Lord was doing. Finally the shouting and praising began to subside, and Zeek swiftly interceded to regain control.

"Hallelujah! Hallelujah! Haaaliluuuja!" Zeek could not take control as he thought, but instead,

Young Darby

himself got caught up into praising God, and began shouting, jumping and thanking God himself. The inspired organist and drummer were on fire on one accord.

The missionaries began waiving their scoffs while praising God. Pastor Gateway and the others in the pulpit began dancing and praising God, and the whole congregation re-ignited into a holy explosion of praise and worship such that this church has never seen. Members and visitors began dancing in the spirit. People were happy. Some were crying. This went on for a while. When it finally subsided this time, Zeek was still on fire with tears of joy running down his face.

Deacon Giz sat there piping with resentment, still unable to give in, so he eased out into the restroom to have a chat with the devil. In the restroom they cursed and slander Zeek's name and his life and prayed that he would be stopped at any means. And Giz made a vow.

Zeek looked out at the standing masses and said, "Did he do enough for you? Its time church that we turn a few things around and start doing a little bit more for him, don't you think?"

The congregation soared with roars.

Zeek continued, "Don't let the world fool you."

The Perfect Lesson

"Amens" and "Hallelujahs" filled the air '.

"Folks if we be obedient and purpose in our heart to do all that he commands, I submit to you today, that we will be perfect as a holy God requires, and he will not withhold no good thing from us, and we will, eat the good of the land, and he will heal our body without us asking at times. He will fight our battles. He will give us the victory. He will fill our hearts with joy.

He will perfect us to the degree that we can be perfect right now and preserve us to total perfection in his sight according to our abilities.

Right now the only perfection we should know is his word as in 2nd Sam.22: 33, where it says, 'God is my strength and my power: and he maketh my way perfect.'

Don't make this out to be some strange thing. Because, being perfect is only keeping God's word. Don't let the devil fool you. Keep God's word and you will be perfect. So the big question is, will we keep God's word? Not can we be perfect. For that is the same as saying, can we keep God's word? And we know the answer to this.

My friends, the first step to perfection in Christ, is to believe that you can be perfect simply because God called us to be perfect, and knowing that it is done by keeping his word. If you can just do this first part you would be already more perfect in the sight of God, then one that do not believe such.

Young Darby

You don't have to wrestle with the question: Do God expects for me to really be perfect? Just turn to, Gen. 6:9 where it says, '..Noah was a just man and perfect in his generations, and Noah walked with God.' Wow! I believe God want a few people he can walk with. And it look like, if we be perfect, he would be so excited that he would even walk and talk with us right now in a more excellent way, while we are still down here. Does this look like God don't want us to walk perfect before him? Now that's at the beginning of the book, but look what it says at the end of the holy book, in Rev. 3:2-6, when he spoke to the church, saying,

'Be watchful, and strengthen the things which remain, that are ready to die: for I have not found thy works perfect before God. Vs 3. Remember therefore how thou hast received and heard, and hold fast and repent. If therefore thou shall not watch, I will come to the as a thief, and thou shall not know what hour I will come upon thee. Vs 4. Thou has a few names even in Sar'-dis which have not defiled their garments; and they shall walk with me in white; for they are worthy. Vs 5. He that overcometh, the same shall be clothed in white raiment; and I will not blot out his name out of the book of life, but I will confess his name before my Father, and before his angels.' Vs 6. He that hath an ear, let him hear what the spirit saith unto the churches.'

The Perfect Lesson

My brothers and sisters, its time for us to repent and walk perfectly before a holy and living God. Make your works perfect before God. If you still believe he really don't want you perfect, read what the word says about Abram in Gen. 17:1 where it reads, '..when Abram was ninety years old and nine, the Lord appeared to Abram, and said unto him, 'I am the almighty God; walk before me, and be thou perfect.'

Aint this somethin', the man is ninety years old and God is still telling him to walk before him perfect. Wouldn't it seem like when you become ninety the Lord wouldn't expect too much? Well that's what I thought at first. But now, I don't believe that the Lord was making a suggestion to Abram, do you?

He succinctly told him to, '..be thou perfect.' In today's English it would translate to: 'Live before me in a perfect way.' I know this aint an easy pill to swallow, after being told all our life that we can't be perfect, as well as preachers, preaching that you can't be perfect. But that's not the word of God, because in Deut. 18:13 it says, 'Thou shalt be perfect with the Lord thou God.'

For here he was talking to a disobedient people who was doing abominable deeds in his sight and he wanted them to be perfect or entirely obedient, but I know we don't have any disobedient people in here do we? So keep it simple stupid. I'm not calling you stupid, I'm saying keep it so simple, until it would be just plain stupid for you to forget. Keep it simple stupid.

And it's time for us to be content in what-so-ever-state we are in, but yet always reaching for what God has for us by keeping his word. It's time for us to wake-up church and give God the glory by our lifestyle and not just by lifting up our hands only.

Not just by saying it, but by living it before him right now. And give God our all. Now, do you really mean it when you sing the song, 'I Surrender All'?

Let's stop playing with God. Stop playing with his word and his will. We must be perfect and walk in the light even as he walked, so must we walk. Being perfect, to God, is just doing what he say we should do, that's all. To say that we can't be perfect is to say, we can't do what Jesus ask of us or what he commands us to do. He said if we love him we would keep his word.

So then, if we can't be perfect, we can't keep his word and therefore cannot love him. But if we would just keep his word, we would be clean. We would be able to live in such away that sin or sickness would be repelled from us due to our clean lifestyle or if we got sick perhaps, it would dry up over night because it would have no sin or real filth to cling to, because sin and filth goes hand and hand.

The Perfect Lesson

Look at Jesus for our example. Jesus said he do only what he hears the Father say, and Jesus was so clean that death could not even hold him. Death had nothing to hold on to. I'm convinced that this is the reason why Paul wanted to know the power of Jesus' resurrection. I'm also convinced, that if we live right before God, death itself would tremble in our presents and cringe at the sight of us like it did when Jesus came around. And the only way we would leave our bodies, would be when the Lord calls us home, and even then he would prepare us for that as well, thus letting it be well with our soul and understanding and perhaps with our agreement.

Then we would step-out of our body, but to people still in the body and unlearned and immature in Gods word, we would be dead, because they would be walking by sight, only observing our body or our shell, which the learned knows is really the shell of our school, holding us captive until the examination period has expired.

For once we are released and hopefully have passed the test, we shall reap the great prize in which the Lord said, 'Eyes have not seen, ears have not heard, nor have it entered into the hearts of man, what God has prepared for those who love him'. If we say that we are his people, in Jesus name, Amen?"

A resounding standing ovation for the Lord resounded thru out and flooded the sanctuary.

Young Darby

Deacon Zeek motioned all to stop clapping but they went on for a little while. He continued to urge them to stop clapping and when they stopped he went on, "While I am out of time and we are all standing, I want to know is there one. Is there one today that would do it the Lords way? Is there one today that is tired of doing it their own way, and is ready to try with their whole heart, to do it the Lord's way? The perfect way! You might have never given your life to Jesus before, but realize now is the time.

You might have already accepted Jesus as the Son of God, but have not been dedicated to his word.

You might have already accepted Jesus, but you are still fornicating or committing adultery.

You might be one that is constantly falling into the flesh-logical trap. Come now.

You might be a visitor or have no church home and want a place to come where you can hear the uncompromising word of God. Then come."

Many of the visitors, which included those that Deacon Giz invited, stood-up and walked down the isle to receive Jesus as Lord. And Jerry was the first one to reach the front and stood by Deacon Zeek.

When Deacon Giz came out of the restroom and saw, Jerry standing beside Zeek with his head bowed down in humble submission, with tears,

The Perfect Lesson

he was speechless, dropped his head and his heart became bitter.

Pastor Gateway was standing and swaying back and forth, full of joy with tears of gladness, as one that just gave birth. Deacon Zeek stood there with extended hands repeating the call:

"Come even if you are already working here on a committee but you know you are not living right. You might be in the chorus. You might be in the missionary. You might be even on the usher board."

Then he looked at Deacon Giz saying, "You just might even be on the Deacon's Board: Come now. Make that decision today people, after all, this is the only thing that really matters. Not your job, your education or your money or your title. The only thing that really matters is us walking upright before the Lord. Everything else can be gravy."

And more came, and even a few members in offices of the church and some board members came forth to recommit their life. And Deacon Giz and Deacon Zeek's eyes met, and for reasons that only they knew, stared each other down while shaking their heads at each-other for different reasons, and everyone that saw this, thought that they had a great deal of admiration for one another.

One of the youth leaders eagerly approached Zeek upon the closing of the service as they all gathered around the altar and asked, "Deacon you taught us without a doubt that the Lord wants us

Young Darby

to be perfect and I'm clear on that, but why is it so hard to be perfect?"

Zeek looked at him and said, "Because people, really don't want to be perfect. We want to do what we want to do. It's all a matter of choice, point blank."

"When will you speak about just how to be perfect in more detail and all that it involves?" the leader asked eagerly.

Zeek smiled and looked at the Pastor.

Nodding an affirming head, the pastor spoke for him saying: "Next Service my Son. So don't miss it."

The youth leader asked, "Why not today?"

"No! I believe we got more than enough for us to digest today.

So for right now and the next service today we will encourage us to chew and properly digest the food we have just eaten, and next Sunday the deacon will complete his points as well as what I would like to call, The Perfect Lesson, the Lords willing. Amen?"

Giz slipped out the side backdoor, but Zeek saw him out of the corner of his eye.

Zeek stepped forward, extended his hands toward the congregation and said:

"Finally, brethren, farewell. Be perfect, be of good comfort, be of one mind, live in peace; and the God of love and peace shall be with you.

The Perfect Lesson

Greet one another with a holy kiss. The grace of the Lord Jesus Christ, and the love of God, and the communion of the Holy Ghost, be with you all. Amen."

Young Darby

A Word To The Wise

Now that the enemy saw ya',
He's gonna come gunning for ya'.
You better not think he's playing,
He's not gonna be passing out candy.
He's gonna make his fight much stronger,
Cause he know he don't got much longer.
You better brush up on your mission,
He's coming out swinging' and kicking.
Don't know what you really been thinking',
But he better not catch you blinking.
While you out there doing your drinking,
That mighty faith of yours is steadily shrinking.
Instead of you being so playful,
You should been studying and being more faithful.
Now I know why you not working,
You busy chasing them skirts and flirting:
 When you ready to be a man and take a stand:
You need to know what the enemy's planning'.
When the enemy come to steal your shirt,
You got to hit him where you know it really hurt.
 Do it by proclaiming your confession,
If you want God to deliver that blessing:
To help you move in the right direction, understand
the message of the Perfect Lesson.

About the Author

Young Darby grew up in D.C., where he attended Spengarn Stay High. Later, received a B.A. from Saint Augustine's College. He'd owned and operated several award winning business such as, The Mid Atlantic Housing Program, The KYD Multi-Purpose Center, The AAA Mobile Notary Network, Moon Bounce & Cotton Candy Corner. Honorably discharged from United States Army after years of outstanding and distinguished service with world wide impact and proudly served the PGCPS system CRI program for several years. But said now he counted all as dung for the excellency of the knowledge of Christ. For his call now is to seek and know the will of God that he have discovered in Christ the Lord Jesus and in this race to make a good run and when Jesus return, its with all Darby's hope, to hear him say, "Well done!"